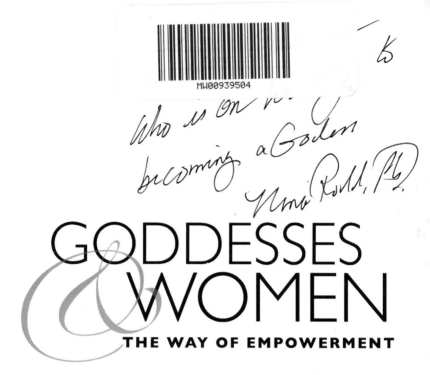

Who is on the...
becoming a Goddess
Nina Rodd, Ph.D.

GODDESSES
&WOMEN
THE WAY OF EMPOWERMENT

Nina Rodd Ph. D.

ISBN: 1453632964
ISBN-13: 9781453632963

The Author

Dr. Nina Rodd is a Psychologist in practice in southern California. She has served as professional staff in variety of hospitals and clinics as well as teaching in universities. She is presently is in her full time private practice as a clinical and Forensic Psychologist and frequently serves as an Expert Witness in courts with regard to women's trauma. Having always been interested in study of women's psychosocial issues, this book is created to empower women based on her work with women and her studies of women's issues.

For Women of the World

CONTENTS

FOREWORD

In relationship with each other, what women want is different than what men want. This is my personal experience during the 27 years of working with men and women as a psychotherapist and a psychologist. The universal culture collectively encourages women's dependency with an implication that male gender is preferred; the fundamental differences between the experience of being a man from being a woman, which continue to exist in varying degrees, depending upon which country, culture, community or family we are coming from.

The extreme abuse and oppression of women exists widely around the world, such as stoning women to death for adultery, or cutting girls' genitalia before they have come to the age, so they would be prevented from the joy of orgasm; which is a common practice in some Muslim countries and regions.

Indian, Afghan, Saudi Arabian and African women are severely oppressed, abused and even killed due to the people's religious beliefs, or due to the Islamic tyrannical ruling systems. Of course it's not only physical violence but it is the oppression of minds and hearts which continues to be a worldwide truth, and natural evolutionary process has hardly helped certain parts of the world to grow, due to the limitation of education and or social-religious pressures.

Psychological studies have long told us that from the time we are born our minds are bombarded with messages that give meaning to the difference between being a boy and being a girl. These messages, influences and realities come from our parents, grandparents, society, TV, school, peers, movies, cartoons, stories, drawings, paintings, etc.

Our belief formation of what is considered to be the reality such as gender role expectation has been deeply and unconsciously shaped and engraved in our minds by the world around us throughout the history. This is the foundation for our motives, fears, passions, desires, aspirations, shoulds and should nots.

Every woman, who has stood up and tried to change these collective beliefs and fought against the majority, became a historical figure and martyr. In order to change the reality outside of themselves, they had to first become consciously aware of the reality inside themselves and challenge their old beliefs and perceptions. Then and only then they could have had convictions strong enough to stand up against their society.

I have been particularly influences to study the unconscious patterns in myself and those women whom I had the privilege to treat in therapy, as well as women whom I have interviewed. I have seen how these old patterns have shaped our identity, our reality, our perceptions and our needs. A programmed map that I would call a complex collection of codes that include centuries of collective unconscious archetypes of women in history yet to be decoded by the heroines who want to free themselves from the daily influences.

In gaining insight in decoding these complex belief systems and unconscious schemes, women face their fears and in order to become free, they have to break the internal barriers; these are the same barriers that limit our individual lives, as well as the true union of a man and a woman.

My mission has been to offer ways we women can unlock the barriers to our inner treasures and use our potentials. One has to go beyond the blind spots we all have, and clarify the ways we can overcome the obstacles that we inherited—just because we are women, and we choose from our true options, not from what we believe to be our reality. As psychology only partially shows us how to bring the unconscious to awareness, I would like to offer the steps that would lead to changes in our insight and awareness, which in turn would change our belief systems and behavioral choices.

I have witnessed women opening up and revealing their unconscious, freeing up the creative energy that was stuck in the unconscious beliefs, allowing them to face fears and discover their own hidden strengths and potentials, develop their new reality, and a new life state they never knew they could have. I call that state the state of goddessness. This state is the state of creativity, optimism, strength, generativity, happiness and, most of all, balance.

In years of my personal and professional search, I have found that the old metaphors, beliefs or "old programs" at the unconscious level, dictate to us through our lives. We cannot possibly be in charge of our choices, unless we consciously become aware of what makes us make those choices.

Whether we are conscious or not, we follow a "life script" that is fixated closely connected to our perceptions of ourselves, and that is what we naturally feel to be real and possible and nothing else.

In this book I would like to take you through the steps of discovering how our life scripts were created by those forces I mentioned above. These forces take charge until we intervene, and if we don't, they will, and will continue to direct our life-scripts without much of our conscious participation. In most chapters I will offer exercises that you can practice in your way to achieve your fullest potential.

The characters in this book may be fictional or their names and stories are changed to protect their identities.

INTRODUCTION

The factors that motivated me to write this book were as follows:

1. I am often told that "women and men are now equal," or "women's liberation changed women's lives." Whether it changed it for better or worse, that is not my focus. Obviously such statements are very naïve and ignorant of the reality of the world, as well as the reality of what goes on in the core of the society, rather than its politically correct appearance. My focus is what has not yet changed in the connection between men and women; those forces don't easily change the inner fundamental belief system within the shared unconscious of individuals within the society. As they interact with each other the inner forces also communicate with each other and create forceful subconscious dynamics in each individual.

2. There are conditions that can change the structure of the society by changing the laws, such as "women's liberation." However, the deeper the layers, such as the collective beliefs, myths, fears, and the collective security system that society has

created for itself for centuries, go through change at a lot slower pace. The fundamental changes can begin only by identifying the myths both individually in one's life and collectively in the society, confront them and process them.

3. In reality only a minority of the population of the world is enjoying a legal and true freedom for women. For example for Chinese women the truth of what it means to have a daughter rather than a son means quite real. The government of China has made the effort to convince people that there is not a difference between boys and girls with regard to their future choices, and yet many baby-girls are killed, abandoned and are given up to institutions. In my visit to China I was told that the typical school classes contain three or four times more boys than girls. Chinese still believe that a boy carries the family's name and grows to be helpful to the family, while girls leave to start another family. Due to this serious imbalance, China anticipates a huge social problem and growing violence due to abduction of women in China.

On the other side, in the world of Arabs and Muslims, mistreatment, torture, and oppression of women continue on a routine basis. The Fundamentalist rulers such as the Taliban in Afghanistan in the 80s and 90s, and up to the US invasion of Afghanistan, would not allow women to do merely what we consider to be the basic rights of human beings such as moving on the streets alone, having their voice heard, or any part of their body being seen. A woman could be tortured or killed for any of these nonsensical reasons. After the disaster of 9/11/2001, the world became more aware of such miserable conditions of women in that part of the world, due to the media's attention. However, the rule of the Taliban is by no means at its end.

4. Half of the human population in Third world countries is oppressed. Women are used as objects of sexual gratification, also as slaves and baby making machines in most areas of the world, usually those needing the least population growth.

5. In our own backyard, the statistics relating to battered women and abused wives are skyrocketing. Women in the work force, despite the laws, are sexually harassed everyday. Only 10 percent of sexually harassed women in the work force in the United States complain, and even less would take it to legal level, for a number of reasons. The fundamental problem in these cases is usually aggression and anger towards women.

This book will address the unconscious reasons that women may let themselves be subjected to sexual harassment or partner abuse.

I witness women and men wanting and being motivated to look beyond the obvious. The popularity of such books like <u>Men Are from Mars and Women Are from Venus</u>, are strong evidences to this. Men are as enthusiastic to look into the individual and the collective unconscious or group unconscious as women are. The reason is when we take away from one side of the equation we have taken from the other side too. Many men see that if their partners are not fully realizing their potentials and are not fulfilled, so they too are not fulfilled.

As Eckhart Tole in <u>A New Earth</u> wrote, "Identification with gender is encouraged at an early age, and it forces you into a role, into conditioned patterns of behavior that affect all aspects of your life, not just sexuality. It is a role many people become completely trapped in, even more so in some of the traditional societies…"

It is obvious that the issues above are universal in varying degrees in different parts of the world. Those groups or cultures that are not afraid to address the issues and bring it to the group consciousness seem to have been able to effectively improve the lot of women in their society and progress further socially, economically and politically. In the continuum of the human evolution, this is the process of awakening and changing.

Chapter I

THE WORLD OF CONSCIOUS MIND

<u>**What is the consciousness?**</u> It's not so easy to describe consciousness, because there are varying degrees and qualities of consciousness that are involved in defining the conscious mind. If we consider a scale from 0 to 100 for levels of consciousness, an enlightened monk would be closest to 100, while a Hollywood movie zombie's consciousness would be close to zero. Perhaps normal human beings' consciousness could vary from 20s to the 70s. For example an autistic person's consciousness is very narrow and could be a lot less than an average person.

Everyone's version of the conscious mind, however, depends on the openness to look inside, on how one views himself or herself, due to the images that one has obtained from childhood in mind. Therefore, one's version of the conscious mind in relation to others depends on the images that one brings with himself or herself to the life's journey.

So as much as I like to think that our conscious mind is separate from our unconscious mind, I believe that they are on the same continuum, and they are in inter-action with each other. What may be hidden from us is the interaction between the conscious and uncon-scious mind, and how it occurs; the interaction of the images, perceptions, beliefs, feelings and what we may call events or logic and reasoning.

So what's real and what is not? What image is real and what image is created by our unconscious and based on what? Well it seems to me that our daily deci-sions and behaviors depend on what we have learned in the past. We would like to think that the decisions we make we are in charge of and there were logical rea-sons for making them. However, a majority of moves and decisions in our life are based on reasons other than conscious choices. Those are based on emotions and mythical beliefs, fears, and perceptions that have unconscious origins in nature.

The process of making those choices are like rid-ing a bicycle. One who already learned to ride does not have to think consciously about the next move; it all happens automatically. When we were just learning how to ride a bike, we could not think of anything else except what we were doing at the moment. Indeed what was conscious in the beginning now has gone to the unconscious mind and we operate from a different part of our brain. A good biker would be able to talk, lift its arm to signal to the traffic, and listen to music all at the same time while riding.

The conscious mind of each individual is connected closely to his/her belief system, which makes up his/her reality of life, which translates to our attitudes and our behaviors. The collective consciousness is a group belief system which makes up the collective reality or group reality and therefore represents the collective behaviors or ideas most of us share with each other—right or wrong.

Perhaps the strongest example of how the issue of consciousness is vital to humanity is its failure in a devastating way in Germany at the time of Hitler's influence on a nation. The timing was ripe for such brainwashing of the collective belief system and almost the whole nation collectively gave in to series of group beliefs and therefore collectively allowed the Nazi ideology to lead to their inhumane and horrifying actions.

I believe that the consciousness can be defined as the ability of a person or a society to question its state of mind, to question its convictions that seem to be right.

What is the unconscious mind? Sigmund Freud saw the unconscious mind in general as the dark side, and the larger side of our minds, a place where we dump the feelings, thoughts or memories, reasoning, and logic, which we do not want to deal with or accept.

Carl Jung saw it as a space in our mind that in addition to the dark side it also contains collective memories and experiences of our ancestors and knowledge from the distant past, and that accessing the unconscious could bring more integration of our psyche and more knowledge and conscious choices.

The following chapter would deal more intensely with the unconscious mind of the human race and in particular with regard to its application to women's historical effects.

SUGGESTED EXERCISE:

1. Close your eyes for 5 minutes and try to keep yourself aware of sounds around you and do not allow any thoughts to enter your mind. After you open your eyes go to exercise number 2.

2. Get a pen and paper and write down all those thoughts and images that popped in your mind and did not allow you to concentrate on the study of the sounds around you.

3. The mixture of the automatic nature of the mind and the mix of conscious and unconscious minds are demonstrated by the above practice. If you like to know the power of your conscious mind to your unconscious, just compare the time you spent completely away from thoughts to the time that you were influenced by images and thoughts. My guess is that if you honestly calculated this carefully, the power of the unconscious comes out a few times larger than the unconscious.

Chapter II

HEAVENS IN THE UNCONSCIOUS

The main purpose of the stories that are told in this chapter, either mythical or real life-stories, is to stimulate and find the parallel process in the reader's own life. So reading these stories may provide a chance to process and question one's values and beliefs.

In the oldest story of a man and a woman, Adam and Eve, the creation begins with the two in dialogue. Life cannot exist without a dialogue, and love cannot exist outside of the dialogue between any two beings. After the creation and beginning of the dialogue between the two, came the curiosity of the first woman of the history about the forbidden fruit from the Tree of "Knowledge." She was drawn to discover and learn, which of course, resulted in being thrown out of the Garden of Eden, a price we all paid for curiosity and independence.

God forbade Adam and Eve to acquire knowledge and awareness of themselves and making their own choices. Indeed, the right to choose itself was forbidden.

Carl Jung, who was the founder of the School of Jungian Analysis, based on the study of the collective unconscious and archetypes in mythology, uncovered many unconscious meanings and their impacts on our conscious mind, and therefore our choices. The Jungian explanation for "heaven" or "Garden of Eden" equals the world of unconscious; a place where one does not have to become conscious, gain knowledge, and consciously decide, since everything is prepared and everything happens automatically. Therefore, there is no desire, for every need is fulfilled before it becomes a conscious need.

It is very similar to be living on instincts we have inherited in our bodies. At the same time this of course would be very much like the world of animals. They instinctually multiply, sleep and eat, and instinctually go through the seasons of their lives. At a human level, our conscious mind provides us with the option to choose and live differently, by observing ourselves mindfully and exercise our choices.

I believe that human being were born to the world, as I mentioned in a previous chapter, somewhere in between the conscious and unconsciousness, because pure consciousness would belong to the divine state and the unconscious belongs to the world of animals.

Based on Jungian psychology, one would need to discover the role of the mythical beliefs in our minds and the effect of the archetypes on our images and its effect on our unconscious tendencies and behaviors. This is the process needed to bring oneself to the conscious level.

By integrating these different unconscious parts that are coming from our shared group unconscious and also individual unconscious, we can integrate the different pieces of our psyche to build more wholeness and psychological health, to open room for psychic energies, for creativity and personal fulfillment—meaning to convert the unconscious to conscious.

It is curious that although we humans might choose or decide consciously, we tend to transform the conscious to the unconscious. We choose to do something in a special way due to our needs at the time and then we keep repeating the same routine as a habit or a pattern even when we no longer need to do it. This goes on till we completely forget why we ever started such a pattern in first place; perhaps after the passage of generations we don't know why we started doing certain rituals in first place.

And perhaps that is the way a variety of cultures and traditions were born. We human beings, naturally tend to resist going against traditional values, and we also tend to eventually change. People usually experience guilt feelings and fear when it comes to changing religious beliefs and rituals. But we eventually question everything, and we always find a way to evolve to the next level. To clarify this point I remember a story that was told by a friend:

> "Long ago, maybe a thousand years ago, there was a beautiful island which was called Paradise. Indeed everything was perfect on that island. The weather was just right, the temperature was pleasant all four seasons, food was plentiful, and there

was no disease. There was only one terrible thing that made the residents of the Paradise Island frightened and that was a savage killer animal called Saber Tooth Tiger. The Saber Tooth Tiger killed children, youth, women and men and there was nothing they could do about it. Feeling helpless they decided to call for the elders to gather and make a decision as to what to do. The elders' conference continued for seven days and nights. They decided that every young man who reaches age 14 should be trained to kill a Saber Tooth Tiger. So the duty of each youth was to achieve the killing of one Saber Tooth Tiger by that age. Each young man's duty and his obligation to his community and his parents was to achieve this accomplishment. The Saber Tooth Tigers eventually became extinct when the last one was killed 500 years ago. Many generations had passed and every new generation was trained to kill a Saber Tooth Tiger. However, there was no longer any Saber Tooth Tiger. The reasons for this training were completely forgotten. However, the tradition continued, and the myth of Saber Tooth Tiger and its fear continued."

WHEN THE REALITY HITS:

Going back to Adam and Eve, the reality hit when they were thrown out of the comfort of the Garden of Eden. Therefore, the human race was stricken by the spell of hard work and natural disasters which by the way it gave birth to conscious thinking and to the ability to do problem solving. The major choice to be made for Adam and Eve was to choose between the Garden of Eden, being happy without awakening to the conscious way of living, or go for independence and seek knowledge, yet face harsh realities of life. Only if they knew how painful it might be, perhaps they would have chosen differently. But isn't that in many ways the story of all of us? Symbolically, leaving the father's house for independence does not make things easier.

The drive was unconscious for Adam and Eve and the consequences were unavoidable. Once they chose knowledge, living was not easy. Now they were in a position to use their own judgment between the godly or evil forces. But then there was guilt in having the choices and the knowledge. Is the serpent Eve encountered when she approached the Tree of Knowledge, the same as the feelings of guilt in our life? Thousands years of struggle was then inherited by man by the choice to depart from the instinctual or the unconscious way, and indeed departing from the dependency on the father's home.

The story of Adam and Eve of course, indicates quite a different process than what the scientific Darwinian evolutionary theory suggests. However, one could interpret the story of Adam and Eve as the evolution of the human soul, while the Darwinian version is the evolution from a physical point of view.

When Adam and Eve confronted the difficult task of living on earth, they were facing the crisis of surviving and the hard work of living. Only in the crises and hard times of life and in transition do we tend to ask questions and find solutions. The emergence of this major crisis in human history was only to be culminated by learning how to develop independency and go through the evolutionary development of becoming a human being, which is yet to be continued.

Erik Erikson (1959), the founder of the school of psychosocial psychology, posited that the individual's development occurs through overcoming certain inevitable stages that he calls "crisis," from the time we are born. As we confront a crisis or a stage of life, such as the crisis of adolescence, we develop by overcoming certain problems, such as the inner conflict between being a child and being an adult and the struggle to achieve an identity of one's own. In case of the adolescent crisis, the teen learns who he/she is, forms an identity of his/her own, separate from his/her parents.

The culmination of the crisis results in change and development to the young adulthood, only to face other crises later, such as midlife crises which forces one to re-evaluate the half of the life one has spent and make new decisions about the rest. Though usually quite painful, it could be a growing and fulfilling process.

Going back to Adam and Eve's exit from the Garden of Eden, it was the emergence of a major crisis that could only be culminated by learning how to learn problem solving, take responsibility and develop independence. This process is similar to the acceptance of the responsibility and independence that a young adult eventually achieves, and also the new problem solving that we do during mid-life crisis.

There is, however, an ironic paradox in the Garden of Eden, as much as we human beings seek independence by leaving the comfort of the Garden of Eden—the father's house. Once we achieve the independence do we long to return to the paradise after death, only to be reunited with the carefree unconscious? In order to do so, then one should please god and do what one believes in order to be what god would expect of him/her. Some philosophers might argue that a human being has a tendency to escape from freedom as Eric Fromm suggested in his book; "<u>Escape From Freedom,</u>" which is also concerned about, the human's true tendency to regress back to the mother's womb, in my opinion.

This is a paradoxical phenomenon, mystical teachers and sages would indicate that by becoming closer to God or Buddha you might achieve a true independence from earthly desires and animalistic instincts. It's a paradoxical proposition to rely on God and being attached to God in order to achieve freedom and strength.

The beginning of being human in Paradise is indeed like living in the unconscious world, similar to the life of an embryo living in its mother's womb, a place similar to the Garden of Eden, where the embryo is not conscious of what her needs are. She does not have to feel hunger; food is automatically given to her without the need for any effort, care, work or problem solving.

The embryo does not know anything about separation, nor does she know anything about being attached, because such consciousness requires experience of the opposite. And because it doesn't know anything about attachment, it's not afraid of separation either. The mother's womb is a place or a dimension where a human being lives as unconscious and as carefree as Adam and Eve lived before they were expelled to the earth, before they were ready for it. Indeed, it is like giving birth to our consciousness which comes with its own trauma of being born.

THE DIALOGUE:

The development of the conscious mind begins from birth and from the very first insult of the outside world to the baby as she arrives to the outside world with a strong protest. The first harsh and unwanted work is the responsibility to breathe and eat. One has to cry and communicate hunger to be fed and then one has to suck the food in. Food is no longer automatically provided, like it was in mother's womb. Hunger becomes a new awareness. As painful as it is, it's an experience that the baby needs; something that she needs to learn, adjust to, and develop to the next stage.

The first responsibilities have to do with communicating one's needs. The next one is to learn to move about and then to relate. To relate and negotiate are more complicated parts of emotional development, which might extend to all of one's life. Simple physical consciousness evolves to a fundamentally complex human consciousness, which is expressed through relatedness and dialogue.

Human knowledge is acquired through dialogue. The human conscience is the next product of consciousness, being born out of relatedness and dialogue with others, and comes out of the human bonding that occurs between the child and parents and others. If the early bonding does not occur usually there would be a disturbance in the development of conscience.

Between Adam and Eve the conscious mind was born out of the dialogue between the two of them. Forming awareness and consciousness is not possible except through relatedness. We learn about ourselves and others and the world through this relatedness. Martin Buber, the great Hasidic philosopher, said that love does not exist in any one person alone; it can only exist in the dialogue between the two. Knowledge and consciousness was born through Adam and Eve relating to each other. Then the development of conscience and morality began.

In many cultures the capacity to develop consciousness is not open to individuals. The culture and tradition is the blueprint of what a person should do at each stage of life. It does not require any decision on the individual's part. All one has to do to close her eyes and follow the blueprint. The boundaries for awareness and personal choices are limited by traditional and cultural influences, whether we are aware of them or not. The freedom to choose is suppressed by the individual's own wiring that gets developed in her culture. In some cultures mere curiosity and knowledge is forbidden. There you would be a part of a big group only and not an individual.

In those cultures there are many prescribed, ritualistic and predetermined blueprints for living, coming out of some form of belief system most likely derived from a religion or a tradition, or both. Becoming more conscious means one would have to question the beliefs that are accepted without any logical reasoning. But to change means altering the foundations they have been standing upon for years or centuries. Such ideas would be resisted since the customs and mythical belief system is usually the backbone of these societies. They take away the freedom of their members to choose, and if one chooses differently, there would be consequences to follow.

In such societies, should a person choose discovering herself through discovering her unconscious, she would have no way other than being labeled as a rebel, going against the norms of the culture she lives in. She may be afraid to rock the boat, and therefore would have to play her cards according to the dictated rules. Make no mistake, in some cultures consequences may not be merely being shamed but it could be as severe as being killed, if not killed, one may be excommunicated and rejected. The "rebellion," however, always brings the tides and storms of harsh consequences in the ocean of women's lives.

A NEW CHAPTER:

Perhaps the appearance of the prehistoric goddesses and deities symbolically maps the birth and developmental stages of human conscience. This is when pre-historic man found some form of escape from help-lessness and fear by creating these mythical images. So when natural disasters such as drought, earth quakes, and storms would occur, they were the projection of the psychological images to the external world, attrib-uting power to certain gods and goddesses. Guilt and remorse were the preamble to the development of the conscience. If then people sided with gods and god-desses, it meant they could then influence their power in their favor.

Human sacrifices are such examples of human being's bargaining and negotiating with these super-natural powers. Being helpless in the face of nature and not being able to rely on other human fellows, one had to rely on these supernatural powers for mercy and abundance. To benefit from the protection of the cre-ated gods and goddesses, the early humans had to also sacrifice something, dear such as other humans.

We indeed created solutions and belief systems and mythologies to avoid the fear of the reality of the out-side world. So we also created the inner beliefs and images to project to the outside, and we actually believe them too. In creating solutions, whether the problem was a natural disaster or manmade conflicts, these solu-tions also created new problems such as the complex archetypal beliefs that continue to this day.

Chapter III

GODDESSES, GODS AND RELIGIONS

Is it humanity's collective need to create the concept of God as we know it in major religions? If this is true then somehow the masculine qualities were pushed to the front and the feminine aspects of God were suppressed.

What always puzzled me was why God's attributions in all three major religions are masculine. The feminine attributes are suppressed or are in the background. For one thing we universally call God a he and not a she. Women are devalued by mainstream Judaism, Christianity, and Islam, and are treated as inferior to men. Though more modern Judaism and Christianity seem partly remedy this, Islam has not done so.

However, each of the major religions has a mystical sect that goes to explore the soul of the religion, such as Sufism in Islam, and Kabala in Judaism. More modern Christianity goes to reclaim the Sacred Feminine. These mystical aspects of each of these religions are mostly rejected, because they defy many rules of the religious beliefs themselves.

The religions themselves go to great length to oppress and take away any power or decision making from women, from not owning their own body to marital rules and divorce rules and into every aspect of women's lives.

The guilt put upon women is imposed upon them from the "original sin," in Christianity, and as evil beings in Islam. Women are considered dirty and diseased during their menstrual period in Judaism and Islam, generalizing from it to the point of excluding women from their presence and participation in prayers, and men are forbidden from touching them during this period.

The question is not who started it all. But it is essential for the evolution of human life to awaken to the reasons for why such things happened. Then we can free ourselves from the conscious and unconscious myths and false beliefs that have taken our freedom, to realize our own capacity in many dimensions, so women's lives as well as men's could be further enriched.

This is the beginning of serious problems for humanity as we see it in this century, creating wars and violence; the global family is a dysfunctional one. In my opinion women's oppression and wars are very related to the consequences of those dysfunctional dynamics of humanity. At the present time forces are at work to cause women's regression and oppression. They could be identified as the fundamentalists in Islamic, Christian and Orthodox Jewish religious groups all over the world.

In the case of the Islamic fundamentalists, not only do they strive to control their own women, but also try to convert the whole world to Islam as the goal of Jihad. That is a large part of the Jihad they are talking about. Some Muslims rationalize the goal of Jihad differently, Jihad as an inner cleansing, but that's only half of the story.

All three major religions have oppressed women and all three do this mostly through the interpretation of Bible and Quran. These interpretations of course were and are performed by male scholars. Women were not allowed to be biblical scholars. Islamic Mullahs considered and still do that women are inferior to men, unclean and evil, as well as by Catholic priests.

The Western world has to wake up from its own naiveté and realize that a very large group in the world is committed to take over the rest of the world, and they want to change the relationship between men and women according to their own rules. They are acquiring the modern technology and destructive means necessary to reach this goal. Even the thought of it, as a woman, is horrific.

Women suffer abuse in religious communities and countries, whether there are laws against such acts or not. Abuse, oppression, and brainwashing are all related. Even in the US we see closed religious communities in which women are used for procreation, sexual gratification of men and are limited in growing and learning, despite the fact that they are "free" to leave. However, whether these women are in the US, or elsewhere, they continue to be brutalized and discriminated against, and this will continue as long as women deeply believe the myths that they are used to accepting. In such inner and outer conditions they continue to be subjected to threat and to being treated as the inferior sex. It's not just the laws or the opportunity to obtain education or not; it is also the effect of myths and archetypal beliefs upon their unconscious minds.

WERE GODDESSES REAL?

Studies indicate that there was a relatively long history of a civilization called Minoans that began flourishing somewhere around 2000 BC, they were a woman ruled society that lasted for about 1400 years years. Dr. Steve Davidson, a clinical psychologist who has conducted an extensive review of the literature, studied the existing facts and analyzed the qualities of the civilizations.

According to Dr. Davidson's studies, the Minoans apparently came from a region between Greece and Turkey, called Catalhoyuk, southwest of Ankara-Turkey. They "drifted south and then island-hopped over Crete-Greece," and apparently spread in the areas including several other islands. The Minoans have been described as "lively-minded," "adventurous," "powerful," and "sophisticated," (Fitton 2002), and perhaps the most magnificent of the ancient world (Hawks & Wooley 1963). The Island of Crete is situated in the eastern Mediterranean equidistant from mainland Greece, the Middle East, and Africa. The island has always had easy access to the cultures of the Middle East, such as Egypt, Phoenicia, and western Anatolia. The Minoans may have been virtually the "direct teachers" of the Greeks.

The term "Minoans" was most likely historically, a categorical term meaning "King," or "Judge," a leader commanding broad powers and profound respect something like "Pharaoh" (Gagarin, 1986; Wood, 1985).

Minoans appear to have been affectionate, gregarious people who manifested negligible civil hostility. Their religion was simple and it was about procreation and fertility and centered on Bulls and a Great Mother; they celebrated life.

Minoans seemed to have an attitude which allowed them to absorb materials and ideas from the East, and transform them into something spontaneous and cheerful (Higgins, 1997)

The Minoan's legal system, political and social organizations were finely tuned and precisely managed. They had flexible social systems which featured a democratic and egalitarian atmosphere.

The Minoan women apparently had a marked prominence and were in leading positions, guiding their civilization for longer than many societies lasted in history. They apparently had a large scope of activity and appeared to have mingled freely and naturally with men in society. They were politically powerful and economically self-sufficient with extraordinary accomplishments, with special strength in commerce. They were leaders and priestesses. They were by all accounts peace loving.

The existence of Goddesses has not totally disappeared. We indeed can find personalities that have formed themselves in images of Goddesses; strong in leadership, creative, generous, feminine, productive, independent, open, cheerful, etc. You can find them among us. We have the examples of these types of goddesses in the contemporary history; some of them are quite famous such as Nan Mouskouri, considered to be the most successful commercial singer in the world, Rosa Say, Coach and author of "managing with Aloha," on being effective and successful while also being friendly in business. Jackie Kennedy who made the White House what it is today and intellectually, socially and culturally was like the Queen of Camelot.

The Goddess closest to all of us is our own Oprah Winfrey, who has been the Goddess of success, the leader of women's strength, and innovator of the culture of openness. She rose from poverty to become the most influential woman in Television, and according to Forbes Magazine, the world's most highly paid entertainer.

I think it is essential to acknowledge and understand the state of women's ultimate well-being which I call the state of goddessness. This way we create a road map to find our way to the state of goddessness.

The road to women's empowerment through the goddess evolution process is a complex one and it needs to first acknowledge the blockages and systemic oppression, and then study entering the evolutionary process of becoming a Goddess.

SUGGESTED EXERCISE:

1. What culture and tradition are you coming from?
2. Write down all the ways you can think of being wired to follow the prescribed life plan for you whether it is verbalized or not.
3. Focus on the possible unconscious beliefs that have limited your life, in the past or at the present time.
4. Visualize an ideal dream goal with no critical input from your mind.

Chapter IV

GENDER ROLE ASSUMPTION

Coming from the previous chapter of goddesses, the gender role in the world becomes a different and sad reality. However, gender role conflicts mostly emerge in societies that are letting go of rigid religious beliefs; the roles that were prescribed by religion. To look at this complicated notion one has to look at the history and the evolution of man- woman relationship and their relationship towards their society.

Throughout human history, in most societies, people have assumed that males and females are different not merely in basic anatomy, but also in the elusive qualities of spirit and soul. This led to the belief that men and women are not supposed to think the same, do the same things, nor have the same dreams, as researchers (Travis & Wade, 1994) indicated.

However, when it comes to the oppression of women, one must understand that in human history, the oppression of women was not directly associated with their biological differences. The American anthropologist Lewis Henry Morgan postulated that the emergence of class society did not occur until about only 6000 years ago. Prior to that there was no male domination, and no property ownership.

It is obvious that the male role has been perceived as the more advantageous one throughout the history of about last 6000 years, except for a civilization that was apparently run by goddesses in the area of Island of Crete in Greece, around 2000years ago.

We know that presently women are often considered less than men in many parts of the world in everyday life. Women now are rarely seen as an idealized symbol of goddesses and in the largest part of the Arab world and Islamic world, women are seen as extremely devalued and more likely as evil, as indicated by religious leaders; the extremist Islamic societies still consider women as evil (Fetna, as a source of evil).

Associating women and womanhood to Evil indicates that something is fundamentally wrong with these societies. However, as a human being a woman is ultimately viewed as inferior in many societies, including many layers of our own society in the U.S.

In early human history men were hunters and gatherers women were the caregivers. The prevailing theory prescribed that men were to provide and therefore own women and their families. Women may have been considered to be the belongings of men in many cultures and in many historical phases.

The differences between men and women always have become barriers between them, which still exists between the sexes collectively. These are the barriers that we still talk about in books such as Men Are From

Mars And Women Are From Venus. I believe that inherited barriers as historical, not biological, have caused severe disturbance in the psychological development of women throughout history, as well as all of humanity. It only makes a good sense that men also were deprived from further evolutionary psycho-social development because of this. Yes also humanity has been deprived of development to a higher level, because there is a lack of balance in humanity; the wars and the global damages we are creating are due to this imbalance.

In my experience working with women, I often see that they are compelled to play masculine roles on their way to success, if they want to be independent and strong, and therefore, they repress or abandon feminine qualities. In the ideal world of Minoan civilization as described in previous chapter, women did not have to abandon their femininity. They were perfectly balanced in masculine and feminine qualities. It's interesting that men too often feel a deep split in the image of these two sides of themselves.

Men also have expressed their confusion about their own attraction to one of the two sides of women and that it is hard for them to relate to women who have developed both their feminine and masculine parts.

This difficulty in men in relating to both sides of women in one body has been historically apparent in many cultures, and it is due to the fact that men also don't own and don't develop both masculine and feminine parts of themselves.

There is a side of a psychologically healthy woman who is free and strong that may be either hated by men in one society or be admired in another society. Even if they are admired, strong women encounter mixed feelings from men and women. However they feel about it, men would hardly trust the masculine side of women and seem to be uncomfortable with it. This side may be seen as frightening, intimidating or not feminine to men.

Men seem to see women either in one role or the other. The roles are either a very feminine and dependent woman, or a very strong and self-sufficient one. The question is that if it is intimidating for men in general to engage a woman who has realized her strengths in being a full human being, what are they going to do when they find it difficult to deal with a woman who is basically dependent and not strong? Perhaps for men there is a fear of loss of control, and loss of control might mean loss of emotional security.

Therefore, men also have to make major changes and make different choices. It might mean that they need to learn to tolerate less certainty and more independence in their relationships with women. With such uncertainty one would have to become more emotionally independent. As women become financially and occupationally stronger and independent, men have been adjusting themselves emotionally and have needed to become emotionally more independent; a challenge that is in progress.

Obviously, a relationship between two complete people, rather than two halves, would only be a richer experience for men and women once they have come to terms with it, because their need to be loved can only be fulfilled by a complete connection, not by connecting one half of a person to the half of the other person. I don't think a relationship is strong or meaningful when one needs shelter and financial support from the other one.

The unconscious patterns and forces that shape our identities and our perception of reality begin their work from the time we are born, if not earlier. We begin to receive the conscious and unconscious messages from our caretakers and our surroundings and later from school, television, peers, and society. Looking at this is like looking at a complex map of archetypal myths and beliefs that are passed on for centuries and thousands of years. If there is any hesitation on this definition, look at the religious beliefs that still have strong influence in legislation, economy, political hierarchy, and in every aspect of our society.

The reality of our gender role expectations deeply and unconsciously have shaped the world around us and is the foundation for our motives thoughts, aspirations, fears, desires and inhibitions in us. Once we face the inner challenges in trying to figure out how we were affected in our lives, we can see the influences and patterns we were not even aware of. I by that mean the decisions we made that we thought we should only to realize later how we were trapped by our belief patterns. Then, of course we have to feel and deal with the grief of the losses we have had in the past.

Though it becomes easier to make decisions for the future once we free ourselves from the unwanted influences of role assumptions, we still have to face many pervasive challenges such as discrimination and women's issues in the society we live in. Let's also remember that the United States includes a collection of other cultures in it, with different meanings for the women role expectations.

As women grow to more independent spheres, it ironically translates also to more emotional responsiveness for men as well. When a woman develops to a true adult level, it pushes her man to grow psychologically. He is no longer a big boy who bullies his mama to get away with irrational behavior. He becomes an adult who has to take responsibility for his behavior, communicated thoughts and feelings and accept the consequences of his choices.

Perhaps this sounds too easy. I have to admit that it takes work and a conscious awareness to grow out of the old patterns and old perceptions. It means that he has to get out of his unconsciousness automatic responses and become equally conscious of feelings, aware of his choices; a mutual journey of the partners.

Although we argue that women get oppressed by men and are held back by male-oriented societies, let us look at the other side of the coin. We need to clearly pay attention to how we women may be equally responsible for the continuation of our own and our daughters' psychological oppression. Looking at most societies women equally participate in such oppressions. An extreme example of it is in Muslim countries where women are forced to cover their body and face; the enforcement of such a rule is equally condoned by women. Women themselves see themselves as inferior to men. It's much more subtle in the Western culture, but it does exist. The example of it in the US is sexual harassment of women in occupational settings that are more populated with men, like a police force, or the glass ceiling in the corporate world that does not allow women to reach the high management positions as often.

The nature of women's roles has changed throughout the history based on social structures. Now it is for the most part up to women to change the social structures of their own societies. By taking responsibility I do not imply that women have consciously chosen their roles in the world. I do mean, however that we can raise our awareness of how we keep ourselves, our sisters and our daughters in oppressive roles and remain trapped in such a place.

Achieving such awareness might come to the individual relatively easier in the Western world as opposed to the third world countries. In the third world countries; this sort of idea would be resisted passionately either by what is called tradition or by religious beliefs or both.

Women did always grow in their own ways, with their own strengths, where men commonly seem to lack that kind of strengths; for example, in the area of care taking, emotional responsiveness and communication of feelings. However, it is not difficult to see that other qualities such as passivity and deep need to be guided by men persists in the life of many women.

According to Karen Horney (1973), the great feminine psychoanalyst, women shape their own personality to provide what men expect of them. She said: "If we are clear about the extent of which all are being, thinking, and doing conform to these masculine standards," we can see how difficult it is for the individual woman and man to shake off this mode of thinking and perceiving, and this is the current status of women even in our Western society.

However, history shows that in long run women can bend their collective belief system. The first ones in history became martyrs and their names stayed in history. They sacrificed themselves for bigger reasons. They still do in the countries such as Iran, Pakistan and Afghanistan.

But for us, we need to awaken ourselves to be able to affect our own dark unconscious beliefs, specifically, those we are not aware of on our daily lives. Once that is established then new mind maps and new beliefs find their ways projected to the outside world and create an evolutionary mental state like I have mentioned before, I call it the goddessness state. This is a continuous work of evolving that has to be proactively done purposefully and meaningfully on a daily basis.

In early human history, the first differentiation of the female and male roles with equal advantages on both sides occurred in the emergence of hominids society, where men gathered together and left to hunt and women and children were left behind. When they came back from the hunt, being exhausted from the difficult journey, men would sleep while women prepared the food. This role differentiation apparently was of neutral value (Habermass, 1995).

Women were most likely attending to children and did networking with other women in their groups to help in problem solving. Women had ample time, while attending to the domestic activities, to discuss their feelings with each other. Intimate communication, empathizing and networking were not what men did during the hunting. For the sake of the survival of themselves and their families, men had to design and follow an organized hunt plan; to not only safely survive the attack from wild animals, but to also get the hunt to provide themselves and their families.

In the era of hunters and gatherers, the woman's environment had the quality of emotional closeness, nurturance, and developing empathy among themselves. Women also had the opportunity to do different kinds of networking with each other and helping each other with various resources. Perhaps, historically that's why women in general have become freer with the recognition and expression of their emotions, more capable in sharing them, and empathizing with others.

For men planning, organizing and carrying out actions in orchestration with each other had to become their strengths. In order to carry out these practical tasks they could not allow feelings to interfere. While corporations more often than not project these masculine qualities they lack the balance of nurturance and empathy that are "Feminine" quality. Women seem generally stronger in communicating, sharing, networking and community work.

However, once agriculture became the main means of survival, it gave birth to the belief that the woman's role was less valuable than the man's. Physical strength became more valuable for survival. Women could no longer be equally valuable, because they weren't physically strong enough to perform the job of plowing. However, the importance of women mainly lay on their role of child bearing, caring for children, homemaking and food preparation, all essential for the survival of human race.

Sometime then women began to believe that men had higher value, since they could rely on men for survival, safety, and food. Well why not depend on men who are stronger and can do the heavy work or, in reality, perhaps there wasn't any other choice. Now women have choice, but many women still function from that archetypal mode.

Therefore one had to learn to leave things to the unconscious. The unconscious does a good job to let us survive without difficult conflicts, so it would make it easier to forget one's own true powers. Women got used to this comfort-zone, in the role of being a woman, where they had to give up the conscious choices. The rest of history demonstrates the consequence for women. There is one quality of women that never went away and that is the curiosity and the desire for knowledge that was instilled in woman from day one.

One could blame the biological differences between men and women for the wide gap that was created between men and women; hormones, child bearing, menstruation, and differences in the muscle mass seem to greatly influence women's physical functioning in comparison to men. However, the studies in this area have indicated that society and family interaction is the most significant determinant of what we call femininity or masculinity. We women are no longer disadvantaged because physical strength is no longer the requirement for survival anymore (except being the victim of violent crimes). However, we still encounter situations where we are treated the same way, as if we can't plow.

Even if we hang on to physiological evolutionary development and relate the gender problems of humanity to biology and instincts of our previous generations, we are now able to replace the instinctual traces with conscious reasoning and thinking.

The issue of false beliefs continues- i.e., religious teachings regarding women. When it comes to belief systems, we human beings have a remarkable weakness for being brainwashed. There are many significant historical examples of how human beings are vulnerable to brainwashing systems, such as a huge nation like Germany being brainwashed by Hitler. This resulted in false beliefs regarding Jews, gypsies, and homosexuals. But on a daily basis, we look at the religious ideations. While religion does provide a blueprint for morality, it leads to controlling people and a man and woman interactions. On the extreme end, Islamic extremists can go as far as to destroy humanity.

SUGGESTED EXERCISES:

1. What was each of your parents' roles in their marriage?
2. How did it affect them, and how did it affect you?
3. What were your parents' roles in the tasks they chose in parenting you and   your siblings?
4. How were you influenced positively and negatively by their chosen roles?
5. What would you like to change in the past if you could? Try to write them down and keep your answers.

Chapter V

THE IMBALANCED WOMEN; THE IMBALANCED WORLD

To be in harmony with the other, one needs to be internally in harmony with both, feminine and masculine aspects of his/her psyche. It is only natural to be affected by the world we live in and therefore, develop only one side, which results in imbalance. The culture that surrounds us encourages growth in some areas and discourages us in other areas, and this is true both for men or women.

A 48 year old female patient of mine once told me:

"When I saw my mother being vulnerable and dependent in her marriage, and abused by my father, I thought of my mother as a weak woman. I devalued the role of feminine qualities such as being caring and nurturing, because those qualities of being feminine, nurturing and giving seemed to set up women to become second class citizens. It took me many years to realize that those qualities don't equate with weakness, and they are indeed the necessary parts of being a woman and a human being and parts of feeling complete and fulfilled. It has taken me a lot of work to allow myself to look and be feminine and know that I don't have to lose my strength."

When one gives up those feminine aspects, one gives up not only nurturance toward others, but one would also lose the ability to be nurturing to one self as well. To be achievement oriented and to be focused on goals, are masculine aspects of our psyche, but to give up the feminine parts brings hunger and imbalance to us, to our partner and to our children.

Similar perceptions happen when women iden- tify with the patriarchal culture for seeking goals and achievement; some women in this stage would work harder than men and abandon their feminine traits. They would ignore a lot of their own needs for nurtur- ance, as if the price for achievement is to feel the empti- ness in the core; this is something that has mostly been happening in women who work in the corporate world.

What happens to a woman who finds herself in midlife crisis as the result of an overwhelmingly trau- matic event, like the loss of a marriage, loss of one's career, death of a loved one, or a serious illness? She most often begins questioning her choices in the first half of her life, reevaluating her life with a sense of loss and grief. It has a quality of loss of innocence because it is as if somehow she was promised that only if she does things the right way she would be rewarded, only to find out that there is no divine justice in the world and there is no reward waiting for her; waking up in the mid-life, to the raw reality, the painful reality and a feeling of being betrayed.

A patient of mine reversed her relationship with God and became very angry at what she believed God represented to her. She suddenly had a serious illness and the loss of health was devastating for her. Sometimes it takes surviving from a heart attack, cancer, or stroke to give way to a rude awakening of how we have conducted our life.

At the mid-life, which may be at different age for different women, depending on the events, the healing journey most often begin once one has grieved the losses. It also begins by seeing the separation from either the feminine part or from the masculine part and how one paid the price in the first half of life. Once the crisis is over the woman usually has new set of perceptions, goals, and life style.

It would be attending to the feminine aspects for a woman who gets married and gives up her career. She may then only identify with the feminine nurturer and then she may wake up when her husband leaves her and or her children leave the empty nest for her. As a divorcee, she then is left with no experience or power in the working world, with fear of being alone for ever. She feels cheated by him, by life and maybe by God and by her own beliefs mostly coming from her world/culture.

This could be any woman who was encouraged by her mother or her culture or both to get married and settle her life, only to find out many years later that nothing was settled.

Now let's look at an opposite situation. Another woman, Sheri, from her young years had gone to the corporate world and had found that the role of motherhood and marriage would hinder her growth in her career. Sheri became very masculine in her approach to life, not realizing until later in life that as she grew older she felt that she had missed a lot of the other side of herself; this is another grief situation in midlife.

The main issue when mid-life crisis hits is that one wants to reclaim the discarded and oppressed parts of one self. Sheri now wanted to connect with the oppressed side she had sacrificed-the feminine. Both the married woman and the corporate woman had to realize that first, they had to develop and become good at becoming the discarded sides of themselves. To learn and reconnect with the lost side of the psyche needs courage and time to process and re-own. It needs time to recognize that an excessive emphasis on one side is at the price of the loss or underdevelopment of the other side. We need to have strong feminine and strong masculine sides in order to be a whole, to reach the state of completeness, fulfillment and balance. The state I call the state of goddessness.

The unbalanced parts of both the masculine and feminine worlds create illness–mentally, physically, and socially, because the pressure of the masculine can push one only to produce, and the pressure of the feminine part can push one to be not only nurturing, but dependent and losing self-respect and self-power.

CHANGING HOMES IN THE MIDLIFE YEARS

Home is where we feel comfortable and natural, whether that is the home inside of us or the physical home that we live in. The first home is often where a woman spends the first half of her life on building her world based on her values, the cultural influences, instincts, or following the destiny her parents gave her.

In the midlife phase of life many women experience a situation or a crisis that makes them look at the first half of their lives and the decisions they have or have not made. The decisions a woman makes can have devastating effects on what she has built, like her marriage and her hopes. One might lose her home, meaning a place of safety, comfort and sharing. This loss may not be physical and yet the change of the relationship with one self or one's spouse still can be so devastating that one may feel like a refugee in their own home. This sort of crisis and loss brings a perception that one is out of control, psychologically speaking.

Once this crisis occurs and the change of homes happens, whether by choice or not, the painful process afterward is unavoidable and only by returning to our feminine nurturance we can heal ourselves. If you have to make a living and compete in the masculine world, it will makes it difficult to be feminine and mothering towards yourself, but the balance must be reached, to alleviate the pain and help you to grow further.

When I ask women who have lost their relationships about the perception of home and what they are missing the most, they often relate not only to their emotions, they also relate to their bodily experiences, such as missing certain scents and smells, certain sounds of the lost home and most of all the experience of relating, sharing and touching. The loss is often multi-dimensional and what takes to heal the soul, is to heal it at many levels but primarily by nurturing and mothering ourselves. It means to becoming fully aware at many nurturing levels towards one self.

RECOVERY PROCESS

The separation crisis hurts even more if we tend to lose ourselves in the other and choose to do that for number of reasons like the nature of attachment, but we also do that to secure our own position as well as to control the other. One can maintain the awareness only by routine practice, because one needs to save the conscious from falling into the unconscious. This maintenance can be done in solitude, meditation and nature. We need to learn to listen to our needs and to recover from the loss of self. We women have a tendency to live for others until we dry-up and we are left hungry, empty and angry. We need to learn how to replenish ourselves by plunging into the unconscious and getting fed by the unconscious by bringing the nourishment out from it.

Remember that the unconscious mind wants to protect itself by remaining unconscious. It is we who should get into the conscious world and get energy and resources. The act of Eve taking from the Tree of

Knowledge was symbolically the desire to know and learn or come to the conscious world.

To have an inner balance our conscious and unconscious should be in a relationship with each other and there should be regular access to one another. The rituals of culture tend to be replacing the natural flow between the two sides, due to fear of loss or chaos.

Chapter VI

THE ARCHEOLOGIST'S WAY:
The Last Treasure

Ann was a 48-year-old young archeologist when I first met her. She said she was always clear headed and knew what she wanted. She never had any serious depression in her life. But she was devastated when she fell into a Major Depression that almost paralyzed her emotionally to the point that she could not attend to her daily work responsibilities, could not enjoy or attend social events anymore, and had terrible nightmares.

She said she divorced her second husband of 15 years two years before because he was growing more and more suspicious and very controlling of her social life and basically made life miserable and frightening for her. She seemed to handle the decision of the divorce well and the grief of separation had subsided before she got to the event that brought her this severe depression.

Her first love at age 19 with another college mate resulted in marriage at age 21, and typically for marriages that occur early in life, it ended in divorce in her late 20s. The second marriage was the result of an intense love relationship in her mid-thirties. Thinking that this was a mature love, she went forward with the thought that this marriage would never end. Though the divorce was very painful for her, she remained functional at her work and in her social life. She mostly focused on her career, teaching in the University, and travelling to various archeological sites around the world.

Four months before I met Ann, she had accidently seen her first husband, Ray, in one of her trips to Eastern Europe, where he had travelled to put a new business together. She described him now as an influential figure, mature, gentle, and resourceful. They connected immediately and picked up the conversation where they had left it 20 years ago. He was married with three almost grown children. Drinking coffee together at a café took them seven hours, until the owner had to close his shop. They again reconnected on the phone that very night for another 4 hours of talk and met again for lunch the next day and continued to talk till late to the night. Ann was not able to complete the project she had gone for, and the rest of her trip for the next 2 weeks basically was spent with Ray.

Only on the second day Ray confessed to Ann that his marriage had been very unhappy for the last 5 years and he only stayed in the marriage for the sake of their children. The feelings of connectedness grew and it was only on the third day that Rey confessed to Ann that he had never stopped loving her. Ray said that his wife was extremely controlling, suspicious and angry and had indeed told him if he ever thought of leaving her, she would make life miserable for him, and would do anything to ruin his reputation and his businesses.

Ann thought she was over Rey when they divorced over 20 years ago, only to come to the realization that she had feelings of admiration, attraction and love for him. They felt closer to each other more than ever. They both were respectful of the boundaries of Rey's marriage, and did not make this a sexual connection.

Ray eventually told Ann that no matter what the consequences were for him, he wanted to be truthful and tell his wife that he wanted a divorce and that he hoped that Ann would consider being in his life. He felt he had the right to happiness and hoped to make this separation a peaceful one.

Ann was frightened and happy. Being an Archeologist, she saw this as a miraculous way of finding an old treasure buried in time. This time she knew how valuable it was. She felt that she found her way home with ultimate bliss, love and peace. She had found the treasure - the Archetype of love.

She clung to the happiness and denied her fears, the fears that only came true a week after Rey had returned to U.S. Rey had talked to his wife, the first day he had arrived home, and his wife erupted with rage and anger and violence, promising revenge. Later she broke down and begged him to stay in the marriage.

Rey was not able to leave, weakened by the disturbed wife and her pleadings, deciding to stay and give it time. He told Ann that he always loved her and that he always will. That was the last conversation they had.

Ann was crushed. She could not understand how he could remain in such an unhappy situation. If you ever felt that you have found your lost treasure and then you lost it again, you would know it is one of the most painful experiences.

Weeks passed in therapy sessions, dealing with the deep roots of Ann's grief and loss. She saw that she had indeed lost part of her own self, the part that she was not connected to and she saw it in Rey, and the reunion with him meant becoming whole and complete again. She could see that Ray had played the role of an external Key to the internal lost part of herself and in fact she had not lost the treasure completely. Indeed, she had not lost it within her own world. The locked treasure had to somehow be opened, but not by an external symbol which would always then keep it as an external phenomenon and not her own. She had to work hard to keep it in her sight, in order to find the connection to her own inner world and inner strength.

As a young girl, Ann loved her father; she saw him as her hero. Her father got ill and psychologically decompensated with a psychotic disorder and was hospitalized in a psychiatric hospital when she was a 4-year-old. Her mother kept her away from her father, fearing that seeing him in that condition would psychologically scar her. Her father remained psychotic, had long hospital stays and eventually became institutionalized for the rest of his life.

Ann's bond with her father was traumatically broken in early childhood. The treasure that Ann saw in Rey was her own lost treasure; her lost love for her father.

The tremendous grief of her father "abandoning" her was trapped inside Ann's psyche and because of the sudden loss of the treasure that she finally found, and it all exploded inside of her in the form of severe grief and severe depression.

Once Ann acquired such insight, her depression began lifting and she began recovering from the grief. For a long time this crisis was waiting in her psyche to erupt. However, she evolved from it by understanding the roots of it, as well as learning that the source of treasures is within her.

Ann's experience is not unique. If she had connected with Rey as an external key to the treasure of happiness, it would or could have faded away just as it had faded away when she was in her late 20s when she divorced him.

LULA'S STORY- A DARK HELL

The beautiful young female patient, Lula, arrived looking tired and aged, as if she was attacked and beaten by a mob. Partially disoriented, she said it was like coming out of the darkness of hell, from somewhere in her own psyche, where she met her own images in ugly and demonic forms. This occurred right after taking a devastating emotional beating from her husband, Mike. He would devalue her, attack her integrity and values. Many times he would make her feel like a worthless little ugly being, leaving her with only one desire; "to end it all."

In only one meeting with Mike, I found him to be unduly involved with his own world, with no insight about his inner dynamics, needing to control and devalue his wife's every action, every move, every idea, every thought, or opinion; he was a bully. The only way to boost his own fragile ego was to beat her down, deeply knowing that if she left him, it could totally destroy him emotionally.

Lula's father was abusive towards her mother. He was a paranoid character and did not trust anyone, believing that everyone had a hidden agenda, which made Lula wish to be nothing like him. This left her open, trusting everyone unless proven otherwise. But Mike, the eldest son of a depressed and cold mother and an explosive, abusive and psychopathic father, very quickly was attracted to Lula, whom he initially saw as a smart business woman, but also, as he put it, "a naïve and gullible woman."

Being a successful young business woman, soon into her marriage with Mike, Lula lost the psychological autonomy she enjoyed before she got married, and soon after Mike asked that she sell her business and that with its profit he would invest in his own business ventures. She agreed without hesitation. Mike became increasingly suspicious about every "wrong move," from Lula, accusing her of having some kind of hidden agenda. This activated in Lula, her old well trained habits in handling her paranoid father, which made it very difficult for her to see how she was trapped in a vicious cycle.

Due to Mike's severe reality distortions, Lula began abandoning her friends one by one, since Mike thought they had ill intentions regarding their marriage. Throughout years of marriage, she found herself very lonely, with a thinning social support, broken self-image, and losing the last bit of her self-confidence.

When she came to my office for treatment, she was caught in a cycle of abuse, having lost her own self-respect and self-confidence, being fearful, doubtful of her own abilities; Mike's occasional short lived affectionate moves towards her made it impossible for her to escape. She was desperately addicted to those rare happy occasions, so she would take all the emotional battery, regularly being manipulated by his rationalizations that she is the one who is responsible for his reactions, and that she is the one who created the problems, therefore, deserving the beatings.

Lula's story is not unique, in that many women get caught in this kind of abusive paradox, devastated by self-blame, guilt, confusion, loss of self-respect and personal strength. This results in damaged self-image, drinking the poisonous life one sip at a time, waiting for those occasional loving moments. This results in staying longer, until the soul gets corrupted by abuse, and the body becomes infested with chronic diseases.

In these cases, the abusive person usually finds weak and vulnerable spots in the psyche of the other and she gradually caves in, like Lula's vulnerability to the self-doubt that her father had left in her.

But Lula did leave Mike. It took another three years after separation from Mike, to find herself again, but this time she had the insight about a hole in her ego, which she had tried to fill with success in her business after she had left her father's house. This was a split self representation of being on the other far side of the spectrum, of being too trusting, self-doubting and vulnerable. She was able to see that she needed to protect herself, reasonably question others and shield herself from abusive men and in so doing, she learned that she would not be transformed into her paranoid father.

Continuing her quest in building a wholesome psyche, Lula dedicates her free time to help women who get caught in similar abusive cycles and feels fulfilled. Each time she helped another woman with an abusive relationship she received confirmation about her own psychological evolution.

SUGGESTED EXERCISES:

1. Relax for a few minutes; try not to think of anything that comes to your mind.
2. Look inside your psyche to find those weak spots.
3. Pick one prominent one.
4. Think back as long as you can remember to see where you started being affected, in your childhood and young years.
5. Patiently watch your life and see how the weak spot has affected your decisions in life; your tendencies and your actions or inactions.
6. Being able to see this and keeping the insight is only the first, but a big step to begin with.

Chapter VII

FROM DEPRESSION TO FULFILLMENT
Women's true stories

Our perception of ourselves at deeper unconscious levels goes beyond the knowledge of the rational mind, we cannot easily access it. It is, however, accessible with focused therapeutic work at the deeper levels. I call some of these perceptions deceptions of our unconscious, because our minds are complicated. We are under the spell of these repeated mental programs and yet we are not quite aware of them in our day to day life. It is common that women share these perceptions with each other at some level.

I have witnessed many individuals who were open to unfolding their unconscious and stay in that zone long enough to understand it, and despite its power over them, build new ways of doing and behaving differently. When we get a new insight about ourselves, it is exciting. Most of us would like to make changes in our habits, perceptions and behavior. The new insight is usually as fragile as having a dream that we remember in the morning, and it evaporates away from our memory an hour later. Our psyche has its own protective layer in order to behave the way it is familiar with. Once we are able to stay with awareness about certain dysfunctional patterns and we become aware of the consequential oppression of ourselves, we learn to replace the dysfunctional patterns accordingly.

In the years of my own personal journey and my professional work with women and men, I have found that the old metaphors, or so called old programs, dictate our lives. Perhaps it's hard to believe it, because we would like to think we consciously decide and create our own lives.

However, once the psychic energy that is used to keep things in the status-quo condition is released, and becomes available for creativity and fulfillment, we experience such results and we truly become motivated to look in with more honesty.

The following story of s young woman could shed light on what I mean by the unconscious deception:

<u>Nora</u> was a 38-year-old young and attractive married woman when I met her. She had become progressively depressed shortly after she got married 5 years before for the second time. She had a 10-year-old son. She never had seriously worked in a particular job or career, except for some part-time jobs here and there. Her husband wanted her to get stronger, go to school if she wanted to learn new skills and make herself valuable in a career, but she believed she was not able to. She grew more and more depressed. Her Psychiatrist had put her on an anti-depressant and yet the medication did not reduce the inner conflicts that caused depression.

After a period of two years of getting medication treatment, she had a powerful dream that made her finally notice that there must be a deeper issue than biological reasons for her depression, so she called me for an appointment. She came in distressed by the following dream she could "not get out of my mind":

"I am a teacher and a there was a little girl sitting in front of me. I felt very concerned about her. She seemed to have some type of learning disability. I was trying to teach her how to write or understand some numbers. An angry woman was watching us….she was the little girl's mother. She was blaming and resenting the little girl's inability to learn, saying that 'she is lazy'. This was making the little girl very nervous and frightened, which made the situation worse for her. I felt very helpless, feeling that I couldn't protect this child, with all I could do to mediate and advocate for her. This mother would not accept the concept of learning disability, and that it was not her fault that she had some kind of block. When I tried to explain it to her that there are special ways of teaching kids like her that would facilitate her learning, she became impatient and angrier with me, insisting on her point of view, and said that she was not going to let me help her daughter anymore. I was feeling deeply sad, frustrated, angry and helpless. These feelings has stayed with me and haunt me every day since that night."

I asked Nora to relax and go back into her dream as if it was happening right at the moment and visualize it again from the beginning. Once she was in the dream I asked Nora to become the little girl and speak out her thoughts.

> The child: "I am stupid, I am bad. I must have done something bad. There is something wrong with me. I cannot learn. I am a bad lazy girl."

Then I asked her to become the teacher: "I feel sorry for this girl. I can see that she is a bright girl. She can learn. Either her learning disability or her fears are the barriers. If her mother would quit that attitude and learn how to work with her, or let me help her, this girl would have a great chance, she certainly has the potential."

Then I asked Nora to become the mother and speak through her. Nora seemed to have difficulty with this part, but she finally was able to speak for her:

> The mother: "Let's not touch the situation. What's the use? Why should I learn to teach her? She is not going to learn anyway and I will fail too, she is a girl, you know. I'm afraid I don't want her to learn. What might happen if she does learn, would it really be good for her?"

Nora could not get anything more out of the mother figure that day. The mother in the dream would not respond to the questions about what might happen that she is frightened of.

In the next few sessions it became clear that the harsh and critical parent internalized inside Nora was actually very frightened. Nora soon associated the word female with the term learning-disabled. She recognized that the message in this dream was that she needed to learn how to learn. The numbers that the girl could not learn resembles mathematical issues, which is usually considered a masculine task. If you go to a math class or an engineering school usually you see far more male students than females. I interpreted that learning of the numbers in the dream, was actually a symbol of masculine dominance in the masculine world.

However, there was something more complex going on; the mother figure who herself had not taken steps to the uncharted regions in her life was afraid of the division and separation from her daughter. This mother was more comfortable in denying her daughter's capability to learn such skills than admit that the girl was bright. She basically believed that way because it was easier to think that her daughter would fail anyway, and the feared separation would not happen. So she would be better off to be considered lazy and dumb than trying anything else. It sounds like a very dysfunctional family and in fact Nora's relationship was a very neurotic one. Indeed, the learning disability was nothing but the symbol of the mother's fear of failure and separation.

We as adults have our parental figures integrated in our personality. The conflict and the struggle between these three sides of Nora's personality, that she had not yet integrated, were psychologically exhausting and had resulted in a chronic depression. This depression had served as sort of self-fulfilling prophecy that did not let her to be productive in her world and made her more dependent on her husband.

The frightened mother was a harsh and critical oppressor. This oppressive mother was not only the reflection of Nora's actual mother; it was a symbol of the culture that Nora was brought up in since her birth. Nora was not aware of the magnitude of its dominance in her life, because she intellectually knew of her choices and would rationalize why she would not take certain options in her life.

When we are frightened, we become more oppressive with ourselves and our loved one. It serves as a more complex denial mechanism. This is the only defense mechanism that is primitively available and protects us from facing our fears at a dear cost. While in primitive societies such oppression for women is externally and internally imposed, in Nora's situation, as an adult, such oppression was only internally imposed.

Nora's dream depicted how our psyche seeks balance almost at any cost. The internalized critical/oppressive mother and the child are in a state of such imbalance that the negotiating side, meaning the teacher, wanted to find a solution. But she could only do this in a symbolic fashion in a dream, in order to escape the walls of the unconscious mechanisms. She was not ready to see it consciously yet until she gradually became aware of her inner dynamics.

For the next two years Nora dealt with the harsh but frightened parent inside her psyche and the little girl who truly believed she is no good. Her depression was lifting more and more as she uncovered the issues and coached herself in learning new ways and facing new challenges in her marital relationship.

Once these unconscious parts were integrated and understood, Nora was able to start working on an individuation process, one step at a time and gradually achieve self-enrichment and growth. She blossomed as she helped the child within and believed in her strengths. She entered a teacher certification program and became a schoolteacher and discovered how much she enjoyed working with children.

Nora's husband tried to encourage her and in a supportive way to push her, but Nora was seriously emotionally blocked; yet the husband's insistence stimulated the disturbing dreams that were sending messages to Nora that needed to be discovered.

It is often scary to confront the inner fears of seeing the truth. Many of us who tried very hard to make a dysfunctional relationship work would know about a familiar pattern of coping in the earlier stages of their marriage/relationship. They would hide things from themselves. They would rationalize the reasons why they "should not bring it up," or "learn to adjust to it," and that "he will change if I only do this or that." I have heard men and women saying things like, "if I put my foot down and confront him/her, he/she would leave me."

But the real reason is not that we are doing our partner a favor by not confronting the issues. In fact we are ruining the chance of developing the relationship to a higher level. This sort of hiding behind the rationalization is designed to avoid conflicts and avoid facing the scary stuff. However, these denied and avoided parts do come back in deformed shapes and obscure ways to hunt us. These deformed parts come back in the form of depression, anxiety, anger and resentment towards the other partner, and despair. It could go further to acting out behavior such as infidelity in the marriage.

Judy, a 45-year-old woman who after a very abusive 15-year marriage divorced her husband, was in therapy for the last 3 years of her marriage. She did not have any strength to leave when she started her treatment. It took her three years to overcome her fears; financial fears, fear of the world punishing her if she left her husband, and fear of being alone forever. But she continued dreaming and planning to leave.

When she had the strength to leave, she got herself a nice apartment and organized her life, but then she began feeling the strong waves of emotional pain and grief. No matter how horrible a relationship is, it is still a significant loss. It is the loss of her husband and the loss of what was familiar in her.

After a year had passed, she was still in heavy grief. She said it was so painful that she would forget why she left him at all. Then there were two years of the same painful experience. Something more profound than loss and grief was torturing her psychologically-a deep feeling of abandonment, even though she was the one who had left the relationship. She would describe her feelings resembling to a 5-year-olf girl whose parents had died; "I feel like an orphan, I am lost, I feel so small and vulnerable."

She had learned about her tendency of getting into abusive relationships. She had stayed away from men so she would not repeat the same patterns; this was a rational decision on her part. Her father was abusive towards her and her mother in her childhood. It was interesting that she picked men who had similar personalities and like her father were abusive towards her. It was an automatic and unconscious attraction to the familiar with hopes of repairing what went wrong in her childhood. She did not know any other emotional road map, while she was very sure she didn't want the same type of relationship.

Though It was very painful for her to stay alone and feel lonely, she got herself busy with work and her hobbies, and stayed away from getting involved with anyone. She had to take her time to learn a new psychological alphabet of getting into a reasonable relationship with a man who would be capable of empathy and consistent caring which was very important to her.

Judy had to do some trial and error in order to practice and get it right. She did get it right, finally, finding the right man in the fifth year after her divorce. This one was different from her ex-husband, her father and any abusive man she was drawn to.

SUGGESTED EXERCISES:

Exercise 1:
Write down certain choices that you have made in distant past. Explore the possible unconscious factors including fears or gender-role expectations that might have led to those decisions.

Exercise 2:
Now write down all other possible choices or options that may have been available to you at the time, if you were not overpowered by the factors above.

Chapter VIII

THE CHALLENGE OF BEING A WOMAN

Perhaps in a woman's life comes a time of certain discovery, when she discovers that the Cinderella Story was a lie, but a woman may still wish that it would have been true. If a dream is a part of our psych, when we lose it we lose a part of our psyche. We have to grieve it and at some point grow a new part.

In such situations we are pushed to make changes. A crisis brings a loss which makes it inevitable to either change and grow or do something that is even more destructive, like repeating the same patterns, because it is so hard to cut out a part of ourselves with no idea how it may feel if we did grow a new part. Perhaps it's too far away to see it and too hard to believe it.

Let's look at the way psychology looks at the feminine role. Karen Horney (1973) indicated that psychoanalysis is a creation of man as it is more of a masculine psychology. It is more geared to understanding mens' psychological development than womens'.

My own conclusion is that the feminine development from the psychoanalytic point of view lies in the subjective understanding of the cause and effect of the female psyche, physiology and behavior. It is biased towards women, misunderstands and therefore devalues women.

This is an old and complicated issue, because women's perception of inferiority about themselves and men's perception of it are different. A woman can analyze her feelings of inferiority, only when she gains a true awareness of such perception in herself, and when she is able to observe its evidences and consequences in her own life. Then she is able to begin changing.

In Nora's case, part of her psyche had fallen asleep as the spell was cast over her by her mother's dysfunctional relationship with her. Part of her psych was awakening and was begging for attention when she had the disturbing dream about the little girl. Here she had to learn the truth and go through abandoning the dysfunctional part which was her belief about herself.

For Judy it took a lot of hard work in therapy to find a new way of relating and finding the right formula for a fulfilling relationship. She used to get attracted to men who were like her father; because unconsciously she wanted to fix the problems she had with her father so she could make this man who was like her father love her. But now she knows that in such a relationship she regresses to being a 4-5 year old girl with no strength of her own. She learned that she did not want that kind of a relationship, it was too painful, and went about relearning how to be in a healthy relationship.

In the old mythical stories of treasure hunts, the treasure is usually hidden deep in an unknown and difficult to access place and guarded by dragons or dangerously evil beings. The hero or the heroine of the story has to first confront the evil beings. Just like these mythical stories the unconscious mind guards the treasures with the psychic instruments that Freud called defense mechanisms. Despite these strong guards one has to confront the guards in order to access the truth deep within. It's like meeting a dragon at the gate where the treasure or the truth is hidden, experiencing the terrifying feelings and yet fighting it, only to realize that the dragon was nothing except an inflated imaginary thing. But this realization would only occur after the serious confrontation with our fears and learning that those fears were the very confining structures keeping us away from the truth.

The reason for many decisions we make or many decisions we don't make, or those we avoid making is due to fear; separating from the familiar concepts is frightening as it is with confronting something we are terrified of. Many times when we have to confront something we are afraid of, we find out that, there was meant to be a learning experience, or a new realization in our life. Fears are like myths that are hardly questioned and hardly confronted. To understand the extent of this issue, just imagine how many myths and false beliefs women had to confront within the last one hundred years.

A woman's love is expressed through the roles she assumes and the archetypes in her subconscious mind that set strong programs and expectations. These archetypes, shadows and patterns, are imprinted deep in her inner world of collective unconscious through centuries of collective history. The effect of it begins from the moment she comes to this world and continues throughout the tender years of her childhood by observing her parents and the world around her, being influenced by unspoken cultural beliefs or false beliefs and blueprints.

Her role as a woman is inscribed in what she sees, hears, and perceives which become her fundamental values and unconscious program. Let's focus on the women of the Baby Boomers generation. The messages were given to her unconscious mind through the stories such as the Cinderella story. Cinderella was a girl who was rewarded for her obedience and her miseries by finding the Prince and living happily ever after. The Beauty and the Beast is another story where the beauty is helpless in the face of the beast or the handsome Prince. The messages are still carried in the more modern version of stories such as the James Bond story and his women; The women who were used by him as either sexual object or as tools.

A woman also soon finds out that women are prone to the effects of violence; they become victims of abuse, rape and battery by men. She also finds out that the world is not such a safe or fair place, and she is not rewarded just because she follows the rules. She learns that men are also fathers and head of their families; boys are considered better in math and mechanics than girls, and so on.

It's not difficult to see that if these repetitive messages would have been different, the resulting picture could be fundamentally different too. These structures and roles distance us from our core, from who we really are, and who we really can be. This distancing ends in death of certain parts of us, which, given the ,opportunity they could evolve to fulfillment within; we need to realize our talents and our potentials, otherwise we lose those parts as if we never had them; I call these lost part, dead potentials.

Imagine how our lives could have been if we had owned and kept those lost parts we never experienced. We have a chance to get a glimpse of it if we could just ask the question. Only when we ask as women how to map the lost connections within, can we become more integrated, and get the missing parts back. Only then does our mission to become whole begin. This process begins with deep examination of early and continuous influences.

According to the psychology of identity development, gender role development which involves acquiring and adopting certain gender-role behaviors, seem to begin quite early in life. By age three or sooner, children refer to themselves as "boy" or "girl," and show preferences for behaviors and activities that are consistent with gender-role stereotypes. Sex-role stereotypes develop fairly early and affect children's play, memory, and attributions (Bigler, 1995).

This means that children are actually affected very early on as to what they should prefer and what they should expect of themselves and others. This is the beginning of the separation from parts of us, as women or girls, that we may not develop further due to these attributions.

Just as any subordinate group, women usually get judged by the values of the masculine world and society. This includes religious beliefs, social role-expectations, corporate ideals, and so on. In looking at their own worth, women had to adopt a series of values to evaluate themselves from men's point of view. A very clear example among women's struggles was getting the right to vote; prior to that it was true that women were in a position to allow men to organize their life and therefore their beliefs.

Frankel and Rathvon (1980, p.386), expressed:

"We have grown up in a world peopled by only men and women. But for all of life as we have known it, one half of the people have been portrayed as a lesser and secondary breed. Growth for the other half has tended to be conceptualized as movement away from those attributes identified with women and toward those identified with men. …. it becomes more apparent that we think of growth, we have been thinking in terms of this mental image of a man. … A male boy is supposed to give up identifications with certain ideas. …He is encouraged to give up identifications with those processes, for instance care taking, which women are doing…. Where processes are structured to limit direct emotional engagement with anybody, male or female."

It is a humbling experience to become aware of the magnitude of the deep influences in the structures and foundations of our belief system. Alfred Adler (1973) believed that women have universally suffered from severe psychological disturbance due to the obvious advantage men have had just for being men in the society. And this has carved deep psychological patterns of inferiority in women.

Throughout the history women needed men for survival. Therefore they had to maintain a submissive role and cater to mens' physical and emotional needs. Psychological studies indicate that womens' fear of success is an important factor in the dynamic of the relationship between women, men and society.

Much of the psychological research on women's fear of success was performed by Horner (1968), observing that women anticipate negative social consequences for their achievement in competition with men. Those women expect to become intimidating to men, to stay alone, and not be considered feminine, while men conversely expect that success would lead them to further positive growth and cultural rewards. This study was followed and confirmed further by Horner and Walsh (1974). Kanefield (1985) also traced womens' serious internal conflicts in relationship with achievement in the professional or business world.

Ruth Moulton in her book <u>Professional Success, a Conflict for Women</u>, indicated that Women have to give up the safety and security of feelings of being taken care of, in favor of the drive to master, achieve and have self-expression. Success and achievement are sources of anxiety for women, which comes from the hidden need for dependence.

This is true if we can perceive how women collectively have depended on men throughout ages. This dependency was associated with such qualities as safety, survival, and support. To achieve means to become independent. The quality of independence is commonly associated with the separation from the source of the attachment. The detachment is associated with fear and unpredictable situations and danger. We need to take this seriously under the consideration that only during the last decades in the Western world has there been a sharp movement towards the growth of opportunities for women. In the book called <u>Women who Broke All The Rules (1999)</u>, this mostly American movement among the baby boomer females has been clearly portrayed. But we need to make sure that we are not misguided to believe that this is a global experience; rather it is of the baby boomers in the United States and some Western countries.

For the above group the transition has not been a perfect one either. From the emotional and psychological point of view, whatever way a baby boomer woman chooses to turn, there is a deep loss waiting, going back and forth from dependency to independency and back again to get what she lost in the first place. What I mean is that I am observing a reverse flow of some women wanting and looking for men who are willing to offer the protection that women used to feel with their husbands.

If a woman achieves a strong sense of identity, as an independent and accomplished woman, she most likely loses her own feminine sense and would be disappointed with the loss later on in her life. If she holds on to the feminine roles and expectations, then she cannot grasp and maintain her own sense of strength and independence. This is the kind of paradoxical conflict that woman today are experiencing.

This deep loss of one or the other side occurs because of the external pressures of society in defining either feminine or masculine qualities rather the integrated picture. Therefore, many women face deep doubts and instability of their own self-image. For example, changes have been a very difficult undertaking for the baby boomer women from social, psychological and political viewpoints. Perhaps it would take another generation or two to settle this instability, just like any other major social change.

The blueprint for femininity is the archetype of the traditional female role rather than a new feminine identity, which is yet to be developed in the future. Women of the 20th and 21st century are in transition, the transition that has created confusion for women and men.

Ashton Applewhite in her Book Cutting Loose writes about a woman who goes through divorce and says: "Having gone from dependent wife to self supporting artist, Winifred succinctly describes the changes of role: 'I've switched from being a service person to being achievement-oriented .' The energy that went into taking care of Marty and making a loving home for his three daughters now goes into her own interests and career. One reason Winifred now feels good about herself is that, as for many other women, divorce made it acceptable for her to explore traditionally male roles and spheres of influence, in her case real estate investment and money management. The measure of her competence is no longer limited to the conventional care giving domains."

In my practice I have observed that women often have a hard time emotionally completely navigating between the two conflicting roles of independence and femininity. For men it is quite different; there is no conflict between a man's desire to be masculine and be successful. In fact quite to the contrary, success in business and career adds to the masculinity, the attractiveness and popularity of men from both men's and women's point of views. The opposite is not consistent with this truth; a woman's success in business and career does not necessarily add to her feminine attractiveness and her popularity both among men and women.

Dependence and ego-weakness go hand in hand, similar to a child's dependence upon her parents and their approval. In many cultures women get punished, overtly or covertly, for asserting their own independence. A woman's success and self-assertion can be threatening to the male's masculinity, and to the other womens' feelings of safety and security.

A woman who achieves independence of self-expression, most likely experiences fear of retaliation from men and other women; As Butler and Giess in their 1990 studies of women concluded that women get punished by the society through negative evaluation, and therefore these women in attempting to modify the offensive behaviors, go to social isolation, especially if these women are also perceived as not interested in children. Either way she would fall prey to inner depression and conflict or the external anger and abandonment for her achievements.

SUGGESTED EXERCISES:

Exercise 1:
Regardless of you are married or not, and if you are married, whether you have chosen your husband's last name or not, try to follow this exercise: Write down the reasons you may like or dislike the idea of taking your husband's last name and give reasons for each answer.

Exercise 2:
Write down in what ways things would have possibly been different if you do the opposite of what you have chosen or will choose to do in this regard. Why do you think would be different?

Chapter IX

WHAT HAPPENED TO THE BOYS AND GIRLS?

Although we know that a woman's biological constitution does affect her body and emotional performance even in our present society, we also know that the assigned roles in her particular cultural framework have far more power over her emotional experiences and choices.

Studies in social psychology confirm that boys are encouraged to become independent and girls are encouraged to become dependent and also become emotionally responsive to others (Miller, 1981).

With a full load of attachment and dependence upon their mothers, girls usually experience guilt in maneuver they make in their lives, in order to distance themselves from their mothers. In the adult years this can happen in the form of unconscious guilt and fear in face of anticipated success in life and career. The guilt stimulates the fear of losing the love and intimacy with mother and others (Applegarth, 1976). This means that there are unresolved dependency needs, which indicates why women have more of the need to please others in comparison to men, whether the other person is their mother or their father or their husband.

In order to pursue her own independence and her own desires she has to take steps that would distance her from her mother, or her partner. And conversely, in order to please men she may deeply feel that she has to deny her own interests and abilities (Stiver, 1983). If a woman deprives herself from gaining work success and achievements, then she is deprived of the self-esteem that she can acquire from that (Person, 1982). The lower her self-esteem goes the less she tries to become independent and this becomes a vicious cycle.

There is a potential loss a woman has to grieve for, from either side; meaning either loss of closeness with the man she lives with or the loss of opportunity, success, self-confidence and independence. She might lose love and acceptance if she asserts herself and seeks her own identity. She would lose self-fulfillment and self-actualization if she plays it safe, and maybe this is one of the reasons for the high rate of depression in women (Twice as much as found among men). Those women who strive to please their men seem to also avoid striving for success in their life.

What we have discussed so far makes it understandable as to why it takes significantly more psychological energy and courage for women to work on independence and career achievements. This is because it requires a certain amount of separation from her loved ones, and in a way for her it would be like swimming against the current while for men it is swimming in the direction of the current.

Often women have to deny their own femininity if they are striving for success in the corporate world. The anxiety and anticipation of prejudice, criticism and retaliation against women is not far removed from reality and the number of gender discrimination and sexual harassment cases in the corporate world indicate that this problem is pervasive.

Girls' psychological development is different from boys, since boys have to break away from their mother to associate with their father as the source of masculinity, while women usually don't experience that early separation from their mothers, and they remain close to the source of their femininity. The consequence appears to be that women remain emotionally more dependent at the subconscious level on their mothers, needing approval from them, and feel guilty about surpassing their accomplishments.

The recent studies of psychological development in men and women and their sense of self not only support the above concept, it also indicates that boys are encouraged to grow independent, discouraging them from emotional responsiveness, empathy and emotional intimacy.

In the history of every person's intimate relationships, man or woman, lie traces and patterns of their childhood. For example the first experience of an intimate emotional relationship has to include feelings of trust and security, which connects to the basic trust built in the relationship with a mother figure in early childhood. An experience, which she/he probably forgot about, but he/she would know exactly how one feels when she/he is in a safe and secure place with another human being.

As children we also experienced walking away from our mothers or caregivers to play, explore and practice elementary autonomy. Our curiosity took us to other objects and places, and we had to separate from the safety of the care giver momentarily till we could build a sense of self reliance to stay out there a little longer, in order to absorb the adventure of learning and playing. Around age two or three, as it normally occurs, as soon as we separated from the mother figure, we felt a sense of fear and we needed the reassurance of her presence, her love and her protection. As long as we felt safe we could separate and be physically autonomous; so we had to feel safe enough to tolerate the temporary separation.

At a more mature level in the adult years the separation I just described is symbolically very much like any temporary separations we need to take from the significant other, to learn and grow further and maintain our independence. The need for intimacy with our mates and yet the need to part, in order to preserve our own selfhood is just like the early years. We do normally enjoy feeling close and becoming one with the significant other for short periods of time, but not completely and continuously being absorbed in the other. We need to remain our self, and if not, there would be a serious problem and dysfunction in the relationship.

So far we have looked at the child's dependency and struggle for autonomy as a normal challenge of development in early life. However, it is interesting that the mother's response to her child's attempt at autonomy is usually different, depending on the child's gender. With boys, mothers are more comfortable and permissive with their sons' attempt at autonomy, with girls they are not so, in general.

What does a mother do with her own conflict and differential perception of male and female capabilities, and roles of dependency and independence? Her conflict is enacted in her response to her child depending on the gender of the child; a direct unconscious reaction from what she has absorbed throughout her own developmental stages of life.

An interesting phenomenon has been observed in the studies of infants and their mothers. This phenomenon is called social referencing. In exploration of their environment, facing an unknown situation, an infant frequently looks at his/her caretaker's face to read their expression in order to determine what emotional reaction he/she should experience. Obviously, the unconscious attitude of the mother and her emotional expressions can contribute in forming the personality of an infant from the beginning of life.

At the later stages of development of boys and girls, Lillian B. Rubin in her book <u>Intimate Strangers</u>, expresses:

> "When a boy who has been raised by a woman confronts the need to establish his gender identity,

it means a profound upheaval in his internal world. Despite the fact that other connections are made during the early months of life-with father, with siblings, with grandparents, even with baby sitters if mother has been the main caregiver, the attachment and identification with her remain the primary one. Now, in order to identify with his maleness, he must renounce this connection with the first person outside self to be internalized into his psychic world - the one who has been so deeply embedded in his psychic life as a deeper attachment and identification with father. But this father with whom he expected to identify has, until this time, been a secondary character in his internal life, often little more than a sometimes pleasurable, sometimes-troublesome shadow on the consciousness of the developing child.

It's a demanding, complicated, and painful process that takes its toll on a boy who must grow to a man. Although they happen at different times in the life of the infant and are two separate psychological processes, identification and attachment are so closely linked that the child can't give up one without an assault on the other. With the repression of the identification with mother, therefore, the attachment to her becomes ambivalent. He still needs her, but he can't be certain anymore that she will be there, that she can be trusted."

This means that the primary dependency needs with the mother figure are differently experienced by girls than boys. Girls continue to be attached to their mother figures, they identify with them, and their connection with them is not severed. Girls seem to go through the separation and the painful complications of it at a much later time of their lives and only if it becomes essential to their development and their independence. In fact if the father is not emotionally available or is absent altogether, a girl may remain highly attached to the mother, and have trouble to individuating from her emotionally. Developing independency for girls, therefore is a different process than of those of boys in general.

The larger the degree of role differentiation between men and women in a culture, the greater is the detachment of boys from their mothers, which creates more distance with women in general.

For girls this means greater dependence on their mothers and a more painful attempt later in life to establish an independent identity. Perhaps this is one reason girls seem to stay closer to their mothers and to their parents in general.

Freudian psychoanalysis describes the Oedipal Complex as one of everybody's developmental stage, which shows up as a "complex" we are faced with, around age four or five. At this age a child is attracted to the opposite sex parent and would compete with the same sex parent to win the opposite sex parent's attention and affection.

This is the age where, boys innocently want to be the man of the house and girls want to get married to dad. The attraction to the opposite sex parent triggering guilt feeling, is so frightening to the child at the subconscious level that he learns to give in to the loss of the love object (the opposite sex parent), and later on will look for it elsewhere in teenage years. According to Freudian analysis this would be the normal child scenario; that means that a boy or a girl resolves this complex by giving up the attraction to the opposite sex parent and comes to terms with this situation. When a boy gives up the idea, he resolves it by distancing from the mother and getting closer to the father. Conversely, the girl will remain close to the mother to identify with her and does not practice separation and independence.

The Freudian view about women's emotional development distresses the guilt women feel about surpassing their mothers' achievements, since they have not separated from their mothers emotionally. Horney (1934, 35, 37a) was one of the first psychoanalysts who studied the female's so called "masochism." The self-recrimination that is basically a defense mechanism against the unconscious wish to destroy the female rival is buried in the unconscious and is tremendous.

Linda Kanfield (1985) finds the Freudian view of women's psychosexual development, i.e. penis envy, and the more reconciled theory of the inferiority complex, and also female masochism, to be very deeply sexist perceptions of patriarchal society.

We can test the effect of the cultural beliefs and the archetypal concepts through stimulating the subconscious, and that is by letting our mind to come up with the first automatic response. Our automatic perception is the true evidence of the effects of the collective unconscious, and whether a man or a woman, we may experience something about ourselves. We collectively internalize our perception of certain roles; the perceptions that come to surface with a simple exercise such as the ones at the end of this section. They could be powerful in estimating the energy that forms our perceptions.

SUGGESTED EXERCISES:

These exercises don't necessarily change our core. However, they give us a chance to keep ourselves aware and give ourselves a chance to feel a new attitude and see things from a different window of perception. The following exercises are very potent and they can be more effective if you take time to retreat and focus on the tasks and do not rush.

1. Write your life script as your mother wanted to see your life to turn out when you were a child.
2. Write your life script as your father wanted to see your life to be, when you were an adolescent.
3. Write your present life story, only to continue the script till the end of your life based on how your life so far has been going.
4. Create a new life script from this moment on, a script that would be more fulfilling. Don't withhold anything.

Chapter X

AN UNCONSCIOUS COMPROMISE

The concept of consciousness or being able to acquire knowledge about one's being and therefore enabling the exercise of new options seem to have always fascinated human beings throughout history. When one learns something about the self, there is usually a price to pay; to give up a previous perception about self, others or the world. This makes it a different task for the individual and the belief systems that keep societies, groups and cults together. The price individuals pay, in their own private lives, perhaps can be symbolized by reviewing the Greek mythical story of Psyche and Eros:

Psyche was a beautiful girl who had made Aphrodite envious to the point she ordered her son, Eros to kill her. Eros went off to kill her but when he saw Psyche, he fell in love with her and instead, he asked his friend, the West Wind to lift both of them from the top of the mountain and place them in the Valley of Paradise. There was this palace where every wish of Psyche is answered; she can have anything she asks for, such as best food, jewelry, maids at her service, and a husband who loves her dearly and would grant every wish of hers.

However, there is something she cannot have. Eros asked Psyche not ever try to remove his mask, and if she tried, they could no longer be together, Paradise they were living in would cease t exist. Psyche agreed to this condition. Why? Because when one is in Paradise and every need is taken care of, there is no need to question anything or seek consciousness (Johnson, 1977).

But like Eve, the first woman of human history, Psyche became impatient and could not ignore the curiosity and eventually she went against her promise and uncovered Eros's face while he was asleep. Once he woke up, he and the Paradise disappeared. The price was paid for the knowledge she was seeking; for the knowledge and consciousness Psyche paid with the security she had found in her little paradise with Eros.

There is always a trade to be made in reaching something desirable or necessary such as a feeling of security in place of autonomy, independence and consciousness. Through the study of Greek mythology we find that sacrifices were made to achieve the security and survival of the community. In such circumstances individuation is antagonistic to the survival of the culture and community.

At some point women collectively compromised their assertion, self-actualization and emotional independence in order to get the physical protection and security that men provided. It is still a common archetypal act for a woman to trade her individuation for supposedly security and financial support. And in reality, she transforms herself and becomes oppressed psychologically and economically.

To clarify this let's look at a contemporary example: A female patient of mine came to treatment to gain control over her feelings of helplessness, insecurity, constant fearfulness and episodes of panic attacks. Very often when her husband was absent and she did not know of his exact whereabouts she experienced severe anxiety to the point of panic attacks. Up to that point, to calm herself she felt she had to control him, and somehow also knew in her heart that she was going to lose him soon if she did not stop suffocating him by her suspicions. She said despite her logical understanding of the facts she had no control over her emotions, fears, and her thoughts.

In therapy she soon recovered some memories from her early childhood; her father was very loving and affectionate to her but for some reason unknown to her; he would suddenly ignore her, emotionally push her away, and give undue attention to her sister who was a year younger. She could never predict what could trigger such behavior from her father.

Looking at her childhood experiences she could see how connected they were with her frequent separation anxiety. When her husband was engaged in his work activities she kept calling him, as if in her inner world the existence of his life could not stay permanent, and it would get disconnected by temporary separations. She had to receive frequent acknowledgement of the attachment, to sustain her feelings of security. This had to be constantly confirmed through external assurance because she could not provide permanency and security for herself independent from her husband. She was miserably dependent, and she hated it.

The new consciousness helped her to be liberated from this uncontrollable emotional misery. She realized how her poor self-esteem had taken over her life and that she needed to take charge of her own further development and grow. In order to do so, she had to resolve her need for external assurance of security. Then she was able to establish a dialogue with the young, frightened child within her to assure her that she in good hands; her own. To establish that dialogue was the beginning of a process of liberation and fighting for her freedom.

When the dark side of our psyche is illuminated with the light of consciousness, we get a chance to have the power to choose and no longer be oppressed by the unconscious automatic machine that makes decisions as to how to feel and what to do; we begin to believe that we have choices.

While this was an individual's story, on a larger scale, we human beings are collectively suffering from the symptoms of the undiscovered dark sides of the collective unconscious; these are compounded archetypes for thousands of years. There are centuries of history and memories buried in the collective unconscious of both men and women. The key to this is curiosity; openness of mind and heart in order to question and seek answers. So we can tap into the enormous power of the other side; the side that goes beyond the social roles, traditions, conventional beliefs and our common day to day identity, and become free from the disillusionment of the archetypal beliefs. The recovery would be systematic and comes in many layers.

Jungian psychology looks into the origin of human psyche. The archetypes once were originally part of human life and then they were forgotten. However, they exist in our unconscious mind and we pay a price as individuals and collectively to keep them hidden. While the early humans had engaged in human sacrifices and then animal sacrifices to achieve security and the survival of their communities, at deeper levels of unconscious each one of us makes other kind of sacrifices to stay safe. Women have sacrificed their freedom of choice with oppression in exchange for protection and security that we received from men for many centuries. Today women by and large still pay the price by losing their self-assertion and self-actualization

Perhaps the reason for this can be explored in relation to what Eric Fromm calls ESCAPE FROM FREEDOM, a wonderful book that explores the human's deep fear of freedom and throughout history he/she has created many nets in the forms of beliefs and myths to keep him/her from reaching true freedom. As much as a woman wants the freedom to be both feminine and masculine, at the same time, there are energies that confine her internally and externally: internally meaning psychologically and unconsciously, and externally meaning socially/culturally/politically/legally.

We have gone to God due to the fear of the indefinite pain evil causes, and freedom apparently would cause the possibility of slipping into evil's ways, so the early human beings chose to go through ritualistic life for the hope of safety, not just in this world but also after death. He wish to go back to the Heavens he once was thrown out of. This is the place where he/she could enjoy as long as he/she did not eat from the tree of knowledge.

Karen Horney was quoted as saying psychoanalysis and the theory of penis envy are the creation of a male genius (1973). In this theory the underlining belief is that in the psychosexual development only one genital organ (males) plays a part. Of course this is not the time or place to psychoanalyze Sigmund Freud, but it would be helpful to take a look at Freud's life, relationships and many reasons as to why his unconscious mind had not yet become so conscious, and indeed he himself was deprived of a clear perception about women.

The mere social favoritism towards men and the perception of men and women's potentials, created an advantageous environment for men's development in certain areas.

Alfred Adler (1973) said: "The obvious advantage of being a man has caused severe disturbances in the psychic development of women as a consequence of which there is an almost universal dissatisfaction with the feminine role."

Although the above statement appears to be a very sympathetic one, not only it does not address the damage to men's psyches too, it only addresses women's collective inferiority complex. A number of other theorists refer to women as masochistic creatures, and once again women are categorized as something less in comparison with men. It's as if masculine values are the only point of reference.

Women have always been evaluated by the values of the mens' world; in looking for their own values they still had to see from mens' eyes. Indeed, in many instances women organize their lives according to mens' values and needs. One simple example is corporate working schedules, values and work attitudes that have clearly been organized by men according to masculine needs and perceptions.

WOMEN'S INFERIORITY COMPLEX?

Alfred Adler (1973), founder of School of Individual Psychology, believed that the most severe disturbance in women's psyche is the feeling of inferiority, and he believed that because of women's situation in the scheme of things, it was worthwhile to look into the context of women's desires and fears of success in the man's world.

It is not surprising to see many psychological and psycho-social studies indicating that women, just like any other subordinate group, have been evaluated by the values of the men's world. In looking for their own worth, women had to look to find what men valued in longer history. During the course of history this has become second nature for women to the point that they may not be aware of it, but they do it all the time. This is an intimate part of the women's psyche, so much so that it's difficult to recognize; it may be forgotten in our archetypal psyche, but nevertheless it is part of our collective unconscious. Even in the Western world it manifests itself when she is in love, when she is dependent upon a man, when she goes to work in the corporate world, or when she is abused by a man.

Another area of confusion is the gender role that is still very much part of many couples' conflicts in modern Western countries. Although the roles are not so black and white anymore in the West, people have to find their own place in their relationships.

Jung referred to the archetypes as a condensed history of human psychosocial development, which includes women's perceptions of themselves, of men, of their own role in their relationship to men and to the world. These dynamics are influenced by the archaic language and messages deep in our psyche which we inherited through many generations that still should be decoded and understood so we get to practice self observation and consciously choose, as well as to benefit from the unleashed energy imprisoned in our psyche that would bring integration and balance to us and the world around us.

Not only we need to individually take responsibility for such growth, women need to do this collectively, to access the collective strength, energy, balance and undiscovered resources within.

Women can trace the footsteps of their own collective unconscious by their psychosocial developmental stages through their own life and collectively through history. Each one of us is impacted by our own individual psychological experiences during our early childhood, our culture, and the social events of our lives, and also parallel to that our world perception is deeply affected by the collective and shared beliefs.

As J.B. Miller (1986) explains women in general are not aware that their other strength is the ability to bend and adjust to a variety of changes throughout history; so we have resilience and capability.

In psychoanalytic school of thought we discovered that individual unconscious material is basically our repressed ones, worst fears as well as deep seated faulty beliefs, which are guarded by the ego defense mechanisms. The defense mechanisms' work is very vital to one's emotional balance and they protect the person's adjustment. Those defense mechanisms are emotional tools such as repression, denial, rationalization, reaction-formation, intellectualization and sublimation. The dysfunction of these defenses, meaning over or underusage of them, would cause emotional and psycho-social disturbance. So the storage for materials needs cleaning up on regular basis. Through psychotherapy, the patient would bring the materials from the unconscious mind to the conscious mind. This process paves the way for the patient's realization of the psychological energy that was used to keep these materials imprisoned in the unconscious mind. Then this newly released energy could be channeled into more fulfilling directions.

Jung believed that the unconscious mind is also the source of individuation, development, creativity and all the treasures that are imprisoned in it, not only from the beginning of the individual's life, but also from the beginning of the history of mankind. In his therapeutic modalities, Jung used not only dream interpretation, he also used creative techniques such as drawing and painting to create a conscious process, so the patient could achieve self-discovery, growth and access to an evolutionary process (Jung, 1933).

Since the unconscious mind is considered to also be storage for hidden talents and creativity, by studying the old mythical stories, we find that the lost treasure is always buried deep in a remote, unreachable place that was usually guarded by an evil and frightening creature who would not allow access to it. One had to really commit herself deeply in going through the challenge of finding the treasure by confronting and fighting the dragon at the gate where the treasure was hidden and guarded.

In order to access treasures we need to confront the evil creatures of our repressed memories and materials that are behind the gates of our defense mechanisms. Our minds are always busy thinking and by thinking we keep it busy to avoid getting into those materials that of course are unconscious. Nevertheless we have the choice and the ways to access them through deep meditation practice and psychotherapy, or through the combination of the two that would integrate the Western and Eastern approach. If you ever tried to meditate and keep your mind empty of thoughts for only a few minutes, you would then know how difficult it is to overcome such resistance and achieve mind-control.

However, only through the inner journey does one find the repressed and hidden materials and fights with the frightening dragons at the gates to access the inner treasures; one has to pass through all the lies, false beliefs and fears. Only then we can embrace the newly released psychic energy that would be available for actualizing the new found potentials inside.

ACCESSING THE PSYCHIC ENERGY:

Through my experiences as a psychotherapist, I have found that one particular technique or one approach of therapy does not necessarily work with everybody. For instance if the individual with whom I am working with is a verbal and expressive person I may have her verbalize her thoughts and feelings, while another person may find it extremely difficult to do so. How would those feelings and perceptions find a way out? In many situations I might resort to certain non-verbal activities such as writing or spontaneous drawings. Then once the drawings form, then just like dream analysis, I would start interpreting the writing or the artwork. In final steps I would try to help the person to integrate such new perceptions and psychic energies at the conscious level.

Sometimes I use a technique which I call spontaneous visualization. It's in some cases easier for my patient to visualize than verbalize. This is because some of us may be able to imagine our feelings, fears and events better than verbalizing them. One way of processing these mental images which originate from our unconscious or collective unconscious mind is to discuss them or draw them. I have found that drawing these images first, before any verbalization, provides a richer and deeper meaning to them; of course, such work requires the safety, trusting and the security of the therapeutic relationship. The patient should feel the strength and support of the therapist in order to face such images and know that he or she will be in a secure therapeutic environment.

A WOMAN'S UNSPOKEN STORY, FROM THE PERSONAL UNCONSCIOUS:

A young woman, **Mary**, told me that she experienced severe anxiety frequently and she didn't know what the origin was. She was also very prone to guilt feelings and at times she found that some people took advantage of her and it was difficult for her to see it coming. I asked her to feel the anxiety while trying to spontaneously draw a picture of whatever came to her mind hoping that there was a way to get her anxiety to connect to the original subconscious material inside: She drew a picture of a young child sitting in fetal position at the base of two very tall mountains while an enormous and ugly creature was hovering over her. The child was very small and the mountains were gigantic, and the creature hovering over was enormous.

The unavoidable danger, feeling of being powerless and helpless, and feelings of being devoured by this monster overwhelmed her. After a few moments, Mary herself was able to begin to interpret her drawing by remembering very painful childhood memories. Her father was physically abusive towards her mother and both of them tried to use her as go-between mediator, and at times they would get angry and physically abused her. The two large mountains in her drawing were her parents and the ugly monster hovering over her was the abusive, dysfunctional nature of the parents' relationship with her and with each other. Not only it was painful to deal with unspoken memories, Mary had to grieve for the loss of the childhood she should have had. However painful the experience of facing them was, it was liberating to find out that she was not at fault and she did not create any of the problems; it was a liberating experience to be free from anxieties and guilt feelings.

ABUSED BY CULTURAL VALUES:

It would be difficult to separate the effects of the society and the collective feminine experiences from one's personal experiences and personal unconscious material. Because many cultures sanction female abuse by tradition, belief system or even are encouraged by their national law, the abusive experience would be a collective and a personal story. The domestic abuse is overwhelmingly done by males against females, and this is a global problem. Often in more traditional cultures, even if the woman fully knows that what's done to her is wrong and against the law, she would not report it because the feeling is that, either it's better left up to the family to deal with than outsiders, or fear of retribution; so it only continues to become worse, as research indicates.

We are becoming more aware of what goes on in the Middle East. Since the U.S. went into Afghanistan after

September 11, 2001, we have heard more about the abuses of so called Islamic extremists towards women. These women not only endured abuse from their fathers, brothers, and husbands, they were also victimized by the members of their society who were turned to extremists-the Taliban, who tortured, stoned and simply killed them. Depending on the regions, the Taliban are still doing the same and are focused to regain more power in that country.

Khaled Abou El Fadl, professor of law at the University of California at Los Angeles in his book, <u>The Great Theft</u> indicated the following (page 255): "Rather, there is a certain undeniable vehemence and anger in the treatment of women, as if the more women are made to suffer, the more the political future of Islam is made secure. This is manifested in the puritans' tendency to look at Muslim women as a consistent source of danger and vulnerability for Islam, and to go so far as to brand women as the main source of social corruption and evil."

Anger, hatred, fear and degradation of women are all part of the Islamic extremism whose power is gaining more momentum in the world and is a frightening situation for Muslim women as well as non-Muslims.

Collective development of women is an enormous challenge that has to be addressed with a purposeful plan of healing, otherwise; the recent extremist policies are endangering the healing of women collectively.

As I have described in previous chapters, women need to identify themselves with both strength and nurturance and rise to the level of goddessness, which the rest of this book will try to explain.

Chapter XI

INNER POWER VERSUS INNER CONFLICT

Most human societies seem to collectively discourage women from gaining power in the world, which is considered to be the masculine world or masculine territories; the territory that men have fought for so long in order to keep women at home, oppressed, limited, and under male control.

It is vital to understand that indeed men and women both have been victimized by such collectively internalized images of themselves for many centuries. These are images that block both men and women from being in touch with themselves and each other. These images once were apparently vital to keep order and survival in the wild and dangerous environment, but when this was no longer so, the internalized images still exert power over our perceptions, which are still projected in our cultures, religions, traditions and values.

Whenever men have oppressed women they too were discouraged from having fulfilling connection with women and a better world. Men also limited themselves from the rich and complementary power of feminine qualities, and were deprived of the ability to respond emotionally, empathize and be in touch with their inner feelings. Both men and women naturally have the potential to enjoy the feminine and the masculine qualities concurrently, and both have been deprived of half of themselves for the most part.

The suffering from such deprivation has not yet been apparent to men collectively; but it results in the poverty of their souls, costing them the potential to grow to a higher realm of integration. The consequence has caused deeper damages to humanity in general.

During the last ninety years women have collectively gone through a transition in their history, and perhaps in some parts of the world more than others. At the same time men have had to accept conscious and unconscious changes. These changes appear to have been mostly desired and demanded by women. However, men had to adjust themselves and go through a transition of modifying their role definition and it appears that men have been evolved in this with less enthusiasm and with more resistance.

I believe that it is essential that women be interested in dynamics of these changes in men too, because what happens to either one, affects the dialogue between the two. I believe that the quality of the interaction between men and women in the world makes or breaks the destiny of peace and therefore the destiny of humanity on earth. The question is not whether, but it is how human miseries such as poverty and war can be healed by integration of the two forces.

GENDER ROLE CONFUSION:

A forty-year-old woman, **Nancy**, was married for three years with no children and a successful profession, and came from a traditional family, came to see me for treatment. She suffered from constant anxiety for the last two years. Although her marriage seemed to be a happy one and the couple cared for one another, she said: " I don't understand, this is the best time of my life and I am not able to enjoy it."

After a period of searching in her psychohistory, we found that her anxiety originated from confusion she deeply felt towards her female role which was projected onto her new marriage. After years of living alone, being a wife was a new role for her. In all her adult life she found herself fighting to put herself through graduate school and achieved many successes. Here she felt she was "reduced to a wife," though she was an active and successful woman. She felt she was a second class citizen, and being feminine meant she had to give in and go along with what she thought was expected of her role, like making dinners and keeping a home despite full time job, fearing that getting pregnant and having a child would only trap her in an unhappy situation forever.

Nancy saw herself as a feminine person, loving her husband and wanted to make a family, but her conflicts and fears were overpowering her rational mind. This was a conflict between the two sides of herself; the side that had rebelled against the female role she had seen in her mother and among women of her culture, and the other, the desire to enjoy a family life, to be a woman and experience all the joys of womanhood. She was devastated because by becoming a full woman because she perceived herself reduced to a less valued individual. She did not see that she can have the feminine side without being reduced to a weaker sex.

Nancy's husband was also from a traditional and an oppressive family. He had a parallel and opposite conflict; he was battling with his attraction to the stronger side of his wife, on one hand, and on the other hand, needing the mothering and nurturing side of Nancy; he simply wanted both, a strong woman who makes money and has a social status, at the same time, a soft and motherly type wife who would cook, feed and comfort him. Indeed, he wanted a housewife, a lover, a mother and a moneymaker all in one package. He too was confused in his role as a partner.

Contemporary couples often go through this role confusion. The inner confusions usually come out in a form of projection. This is where the couples find themselves in a quite different dimension which they did not envision such inner conflicts before they got married. Couples often say: "We had talked about this before we got married and we already had settled these issues." So what happened? They did not know that so much of our inner hidden issues surrounding our inner images could get activated only after we are well into a marriage, and not before then.

The territory that a woman has inherited as her collective unconscious is an unknown one until she goes through the journey I call the journey of becoming a goddess. When we commit to undergo this journey, we would be able to see the symbolic manifestations of the archetypal issues if we observe closely. These symbolic manifestations do emerge in disguise in our dreams, in our free drawings and free associations.

In her psychotherapy, Nancy was able to explore her dreams, her conflicts, and her spontaneous images. Freudian psychoanalysts have their patients do free association, and Jungian therapists have their patients draw pictures, and I often have my patient to engage in spontaneous imagination, either draw the images afterward or describe them in detail by the patient. Then I have them to tell me what they think of these images and drawings.

Fear of losing her animus (the male side of a woman according to the Jungian psychology), Nancy was led to fear becoming a devalued female, which had devastated her and caused her a lot of anxiety. This meant that she was afraid to let herself freely experience what she considered to be a woman and being feminine, and that was the core of the problem; what she considered to be a woman.

After a long period of dealing with the images finally one day she spontaneously drew an image of a woman who had two sides that were perfectly balanced; one side was a very feminine image and the other side was a very masculine one perfectly fitting one another like the symbol of yin-yang of the Eastern philosophy. That was the breakthrough.

Nancy discovered that she did not have to give up the joy of being a woman, while she did not have to lose benefits of masculine side of her. That brought her strength, assertiveness, and decisiveness. She deeply understood those were both sides that could be connected and coexist.

WOMEN'S EVOLUTIONARY PATH:

So far this book has tried to deal with women's inner conflicts, which I believe these conflicts affect all of humanity. Whatever affects one half of the population of any society, will inevitably affect the quality of life of the other half as well as all. The more we balance the inner world and outer energies of women and men, the more the equilibrium spreads peace and happiness in the world.

The family unit, the smallest unit of each society, functions as the foundation for larger society, and there are vast factors in society that affects the family unit. This would make a large list; beliefs of a society, traditions, religion, education, government supported programs and assistance, etc. One thing is clear that a family functions according to the roles that are instilled in the shared unconscious and the values of a society; the balances between men and women would be the strength of the foundation of society at large.

Religion has always historically imposed set of rules for gender roles in the family and between couples.

Women's roles in their relationship with men and society have been for the most part extremely oppressive in all major religions. To consciously change the way we function, means to question why we do things the way we do and why we believe in the things we believe in. Shedding light on these conflicting issues and paradoxes indeed clarifies the reasons why women and men have universally struggled in relationship to each other for centuries if not thousands of years.

The evolutionary path has occurred with varying speed and intensity throughout history in different regions of the world. This varying speed depended upon the emergence of religions, social, economical, political conditions of time spheres and places. This evolutionary direction is collectively occurring, that is affecting the global picture of our universe. In many situations social structures reinforce and insist on certain values that may not be in the best interest of women's development and therefore for the world in general.

What can women choose? It all depends on:

1. Whether they are aware of their real choices, and they can be helped to see their own choices.

2. If they are aware of their choices, then do the social/political/economical/religious structures allow changes that are paradoxical to the foundation of such structures? For instance, in dictatorial or religiously dictatorial societies such choices are blocked and therefore very natural progress is blocked.

3. Once awareness and choices are available in a society, there are evolutionary sequential layers

that have to take place to warrant further development. Awareness and freedom to choose are only the factors that provide opportunity in our environment. The changes also need to be chosen based on awareness and purposeful activities. In other words, if it would be up to a random change, the result could be unstable.

4. A purposeful direction need not block the freedom, though it provides consciousness, self-actualization and individuation.

SUGGESTED EXERCISE:

Take a few minutes to observe your own thoughts, preferably about 20 minutes. Keep a pad of paper and pen close. Write down the thoughts that emerge in your mind and that you feel the need to remember them. After you make a note of them you can let go of the thoughts and observe the developing process. Notice that the inner thoughts and perceptions are products of your life history and events. The true you in the here and now who is fully conscious is the observer. As long as the observer is consciously aware of observing and noticing thoughts, feelings and perceptions, she is in charge.

Take as much time as you can to observe your thoughts, feelings and perceptions. After you stop this process take a few minutes to take notes of important things you noticed during the observation session. I recommend this practice on daily basis.

Chapter XII

GERERATIONS IN CONFLICT COLLECTIVE ARCHETYPAL FAMILY

The energy of relationship between two (a couple) is created by presence of a dynamic exchange of perceptions. A simple physical fact is that energy does not die but it transforms. Conflicts between two people are created due to their perceptions of themselves and the other. Such conflicts have energies that do not die and affect the quality of the relationship between the two, and its evolutionary path either goes to further growth or the extinction of their relationship: That is, the relationship is either enhancing due to a healthy resolution, or undermined due to unresolved unconscious issues.

Perceptions which create positive or negative qualities in a relationship could come from the individuals' childhood experiences that unconsciously affect their perceptions of their mates, or originate from the collective unconscious. That means the unconscious perceptions come from the historical and cultural background that affect the dynamics of the relationship. Not only our perceptions are influenced by our own individual past, they are also affected by our collective past of many generations inherited in our shared unconscious.

If we return to my definition of the energy in any relationship, which is created by the presence of the dynamic exchange of a couple's perceptions, one can then imagine the multidimensional energy exchanges in any single given time at every layer of the relationship between the two.

These multidimensional dynamic exchanges of energy between individuals are normally unconscious. One very powerful dimension here is the collective unconscious influencing the role expectations of self and other.

The tension between men and women collectively could reach a peaceful union if men and women could negotiate and come to terms with family, society, economical and political dimensions.

As we know in the psychology of relationships, it is essential to resolve and negotiate conflicts as they become the focus of the conscious mind. Having that in mind, the shared conflicts inherited by each one of us through the collective unconscious, may not come to the consciousness. They contribute to perceptions and therefore the energy exchange between a man and a woman. These are set unconscious metaphors that as long as they are kept in the unconscious, they remain powerful.

Mo was a young pilot who was born in the Arab culture and had a generational legacy about a woman's passive role as a wife. He became educated in the West during his college and professional training and he decided to stay in the U.S.A. He discovered that the idea of men and women being equally independent and having equal rights was an ideal picture. He genuinely thought and believed he was a liberal man and truly had revised his earlier programming about family structures that he was brought up with. He was socially and personally sophisticated and bright.

Mo met an American born woman, Emily, who was a professional hospitality specialist in a luxury hotel. While they were dating, everything felt just right to both of them. The engagement and all the time before marriage were just great, as they described.

However, after the wedding something changed, as if some buttons they were not aware of were pressed. He assumed the role of the decision maker and the "man of the house;" it was so natural and unconscious that he did not even notice it. His wife, Emily, however, felt very uncomfortable and brought it up in a discussion, but he began feeling very insulted and angry.

They both decided that they needed help; the struggles of the deeper metaphoric layers had to be brought up to light to see where they were coming from. This was not easy but they were able to negotiate and learn how to observe themselves, communicate and not get alienated from each other; instead they saw how each one was affected within themselves.

Mo and Emily, for example, needed to deal with this aspect of their dynamic relationship; Mo had to see that he is still affected by his background and his first step was to acknowledge it. No matter what we think we know our partners, after getting married the dynamics change, because then we are in a new sphere where dormant perceptions, needs and expectations get activated. Every new change such as the arrival of a child can activate some other perceptions and first step in attempting to resolve the conflicts is to acknowledge the perceptions, no matter how ridiculous they seem.

Going back to the collective conflicts between men and women in the societies, there is a need for the modern world to collectively bring out these centuries old conflicts, understand them, acknowledge them and resolve them, so men and women can really join together for the purpose of a balanced and peaceful world.

Just like a child going through developmental stages of growth physically and psychologically, human beings have also collectively gone through their own very uneven evolution. This evolutionary development just as it happened in science, philosophy, humanities and technology, needs to also happen in psycho-historical development of the world.

Ken Wilber, philosopher of our time in his book, Sex, Ecology, Spirituality, refers to this evolutionary development as a chronological movement throughout history as the human mind goes through chronological stages from archaic, magic, mythic, and finally to mental. If we are in mental stage, then we need to strive to a stage of balance. Perhaps, we can have a chance of healing the collective relationship between men and women in the world.

In Western countries as well as some other cultures there is continuous evolution of male and female relationship. The dialogue between men and women is like a dance in that both a man and a woman move in harmony with each other. It's a duet that is played being in tune with each other. Love can be described as a deep concern for the other and compassion for the experiences and feelings of the other, and it cannot develop when there is a vast difference in the perceptions of the two.

With regard to women in the world, the majority is not enjoying the idealized American image that we have with options and opportunities we enjoy for further self-actualization; indeed there is a lot of room to grow, even in the American society. There is no question that there is a need for an upward evolutionary development for women's identity globally.

Actually the majority of women in the world are functioning from the level of continuous oppression. They are treated as second class citizens and they have accepted it. Indeed, our own Western country is home to many women who are coming from such cultures and they have to adjust, learn and grow in this environment. It is a fast forward learning that may be uneven and while adjusting their perception and values, often these women experience pain and anguish.

It is in the nature of human beings to adjust to a new environment through acceptance of new belief system. Unfortunately, if such a belief system is oppressive, like some Muslim states that now more than ever are forcing women to live their lives according to the set of oppressive rules, the adjustment goes backward.

The young American daughters who were abducted by their own Arab born fathers and were taken to their birth country, after many years were finally interviewed in 2002 in the American Embassy in Saudi Arabia, when they were given the option to return to the USA to their own mothers; they refused and said they were happy where they were. This is a good demonstration of the power of brainwashing that these societies have on women, as well as men. One can adapt to the Western culture or adapt in the opposite direction, which unfortunately is oppression.

In another incident in 2002, the Saudi girls who were students in a boarding school died in a fire. When these girls were trying to get out of the building, the Muslim Authorities forced them to return to the burning building because they did not have the prescribed Islamic headcover (they did not have time to cover themselves). These Islamic police did not allow the Fire Department Officers to go in the building because they were men and could not be at the presence of these girls. These girls never came back; their lives were less important than the belief that they should not have been seen by men.

Justice is based upon our perception and our interpretation, depending on what kind of belief system we choose to adapt to. When we lose sight of fundamental human values, justice for women can be different from justice for men.

In a dictatorship-religious community a woman can be buried live up to her waist and then is stoned to death for committing adultery. In fact, in the eyes of the Islamic brainwashed mind all women in the Western world are dirty adulterers who probably, according to them, should be converted or killed; their lives would not be valued if it was up to the Islamic clergymen. Therefore, you can only imagine what the goal of Jihad could be when it comes to cleansing the Western world if these Mullahs' get any power in the Western world; this is something that they are aspiring for.

If there would ever be a change of power in the Western world as is dreamed by the Islamic fundamentalist groups and terrorist desire, what would happen to the lives of women? It did happen in the modern Iran in 1979, and also in Afghanistan around the same time. Women in these countries previously had the option to live their lives more like women in the Western world, to get educated, get jobs and have freedom of choice. After the extremists took over Afghani women were reduced to slaves and prisoners in their own homes and were tortured and killed if they did not follow the strict oppressive rules.

We should not dismiss the possibility of such backward movement in the Western countries. I personally have noticed a growing numbers of mosques in Southern California. Should we be concerned? We should. I see more women with Islamic covers in Los Angeles than ever before. Does this mean that we have more Muslim fundamentalist women moving to Los Angeles, or is there a deliberate movement to influence Western women? I think there is a deliberate and systemic program on the part of Islamic fundamentalists in this regard, particularly when you see the growing number of mosques in the United States.

So having this unfortunate truth in sight, we need to solidify the position of women as goddess-like, creatures of balance and strength, creativity, nurturance and confidence. Such a stage can be realized by women who, once have explored their unconscious, shared beliefs, would be ready to adopt the goddess qualities such as the Minoan women in prehistoric times, who were resilient and lived in a culture that lived longer than any civilization.

Chapter XIII

JOURNEY TO THE UNCOUNSCIOUS TOWARD THE IDEAL UNION

The awakening woman is the one who knows she is touched with the universal history, cultural values and shared archetypes, and knows their impact on her life now and the elements preventing her from making changes. She is also aware that she would have to face these conflicts.

To grow further one has to go through an awakening state from the effect of those many factors that we have talked about so far. To briefly remind the reader, here is a brief list of these powerful factors:

1. Early life cultural effects.
2. Mother's attitude about one's femininity.
3. Mother's attitude about her daughter's femininity.
4. Father's attitude about the mother's femininity.
5. Father's attitude towards his daughter's femininity.
6. The effect of the school culture.

7. The teachers' attitudes.
8. The social-political structure.
9. The legal structure.
10. The extended family's attitude towards femininity and masculinity and role assignment.
11. Media's effect while growing up.
12. The attitude of the most influential people in childhood and teens years and their attitude about their own femininity and masculinity.
13. The accomplishments in the lives of the most influential people and the role models in their own lives.
14. The relationship between parents.
15. The books and stories read in childhood and teens years.
16. The personal dreams and images of the opposite sex.
17. The images about one's self in future.
18. Childhood heroes.
19. Religious beliefs.
20. Religious beliefs of parents.
21. Community's influences.
22. Important events in life and their connotations.
23. Cultural factors in general.

The list can go on and on. Each factor can be discussed in many books. It's not easy to escape from the shared unconscious beliefs that are formed from the moment we are born to our and universal world.

The Journey to the unconscious is a series of trips to explore and find the most influential materials in our life in the form of complexes and deep beliefs, fears and perceptions. These so called trips are commonly occurring events in the psychotherapeutic process, but in my opinion it's also a daily observation of these influences that keeps them in check and keeps us in charge.

In addition to therapy I have found that building a daily habit of sitting in meditation and examining our daily life, beliefs, goals and perceptions is vital to this continues exploration. Because that's the time we involve ourselves in transforming our fate to a purposeful destination, then we strive not to be primarily controlled by the influences of what society has programmed us to be, and that includes our relationship with the opposite sex as well as the entities that we come to contact with, like employers and organizations.

We can transform what seems to be fate, to a purposeful and meaningful direction by finding what we are slave to (old perceptions, beliefs and habits) and what we can choose to be.

Let's consider relationship with men; the union of a man and a woman the mathematical and logical rules are not relevant, such as an equation like this: 1 (man) + 1 (woman) = 2 (couple) is not an accurate equation according to Family Systems Theory. It actually works this way: 1 (woman) + 1 (man) = 3. Three is the combination of two, man and woman, and another entity called relationship that is believed to have the life of its own. The behaviors and dynamics of each person contribute to the wellness or the dysfunctionality of this third entity-relationship.

The dynamics of the larger families follow such law as well. That means that if there is a child involved the number of relationship entities increase such as this: 1 (mother) + 1 (father) + 1 (child) = 6 entities. If you add the extended family then you have much larger and more complicated dynamics. This means if you analyze each relationship and how each affects the other ones, then you can appreciate the family dynamics and also what is called family dysfunctional relationships. Dysfunctional relationships are not limited to families; they go on to the corporate world, as well as governmental organizations and larger societies; then you also can imagine a whole city and a country and the complexity of the interactions of all these relationships.

With all the complexities, it is actually lucky that the world still continues to exist. The world's relationships depend on so many variables, that it is impossible to mathematically calculate the number of the variables contributing to the stability or instability of the relationships between societies.

A woman's place in the world or her place in her own world depends on so many factors such as not only her life history, also the state of the world, the social, historical, legal, economical, power balance and power struggles of the world around her and beyond.

In our imbalanced world culture we also have imbalanced women who try to fit in the picture. To be in harmony with another, one needs to be internally in harmony with both feminine and masculine aspects of her psyche, and it is the same for a society. A society too needs to be in harmony with the femininity and masculinity of its functions; it is natural to be affected by the world we live in and grow only on one side at the price of the other.

A 48 year old woman told me that "when I saw my mother being vulnerable and weak and subjected to abuse by my father, I somewhat devalued the feminine role, which now I understand is the nurturing and loving aspect of me toward myself and others." When one gives up this aspect of herself, she not only gives up the nurturance to others but also towards one's self. To be achievement and goal oriented is considered a masculine aspect of our psyche, and yet to give up the feminine part brings hunger and imbalance to one's self and to one's partner.

It is a natural process for women on their way to actualizing the masculine side to identify themselves with masculine qualities. Some women in this stage would work harder than men and would ignore a lot of their own needs for nurturance. The price for achievement becomes the state of emptiness in the core, because something is missing and that is the balance.

Like men, women also experience midlife crisis that can be an overwhelmingly traumatic experience which might happen simultaneously with the loss of marriage, loss of one's career, or death of a loved one, etc. Women in this stage begin questioning their choices in halfway through life, reevaluating their lives with a sense of loss or loss of their innocence; waking up to the raw reality, painfully finding out that life has somehow betrayed them.

A patient of mine reversed her relationship with God and became very angry due t the loss of health was devastating for her. At mid-life, which may be at different ages for different women, the healing journey may begin, by experiencing the separation from either the feminine part or from the masculine part.

It would be the feminine aspect for a woman who gets married and gives up her career or her choice of continuing education and only identifies with the feminine nurturer and finally rudely wakes up when her husband leaves her. She is left as a divorcee with no experience or power in the working world. She feels cheated by him, but most importantly betrayed by herself. This could be the woman who was encouraged by her mother or her culture or both to get married and settle her life, only to find out many years later that nothing was settled.

It would be the masculine side for a woman who focused only on strength rather than a balanced life. A woman who from a young age went to the corporate world, and had found the role of motherhood and marriage an obstacle to her growth in her corporate career, and became very masculine in her approach to life and found in her midlife crisis that she was missing out on something she did not think to be important before. The corporate culture would hardly encourage women to use all their capacities but you are either this or the other.

In the mid-life crisis, a time comes to reclaim the discarded parts of self, and learn to be in touch with the side that a woman has partially or mostly sacrificed. This begins with learning how to become a good mother towards one's self. To learn we need to reconnect with the lost side of the psyche, because one needs courage and time. Time is needed to recognize the excessive emphasis on one side at the expense of loss or under-development of the other side. We need to have strong feminine and strong masculine sides integrated in order to be a whole, and achieve the state of godessness.

The unbalanced parts of the masculine and feminine worlds create illness, mentally and physically, because the pressure of masculine can push one only to produce in the corporate world and the pressure of the feminine part can push one to be weak and dependent in the world of the masculine.

Let's go back to the man- woman- relationship- equation discussed earlier; the third entity, meaning their relationship. That entity is a bag full of things each person brings to the relationship, including the interaction between their belief systems, their values, their realities, their perception of themselves, of each other, of their relationships, and their expectation of the coupleness.

Inside the bag, there are other things hidden such as Unconscious beliefs, collective unconscious material relating to the ancestors and a history that influences every aspect of a relationship. The more unconscious these energy-producing factors are, the more powerful they are. This is why people cannot simply will to have a good relationship, to appreciate each other, under-stand each other or love each other. The power of the personal and collective unconscious go beyond that.

For our earth to find peace and balance, we simply should purposefully work on promoting women's awareness, and balancing the relationship between men and women at the universal level. This is discussed further in the next chapter.

Chapter XIV

EVOLUTION OF WOMEN'S POWER BECOMING GODDESSES

I would like to propose the idea of the evolutionary process in three dimensions for the human universe:

1. The developmental process of women.
2. The developmental process of men.
3. The evolutional development of male and female relationships.

So far, the previous chapters have covered the developmental process of women, and touched upon the evolution of the relationship between men and women. Although, the developmental process of men has not been the direct focus of this book, I believe the evolutionary process of one is closely related to the other. However, I would like to condense the women's evolutionary process in a form of developmental stages as follows.

WOMEN'S EVOLUTIONARY GODDESS DEVELOPMENT PROCESS:

For a woman, the challenge of evolving is to deal with two kinds of processes to truly actualize her inner potential for further growth:

1. To clear her personal unconscious, which means to look deeply into the psyche, when dealing with personal conflicts. (a) To find piece by piece the defective and missing parts from childhood; (b) to own the defective parts by intimately knowing them; and (c) to make peace with them. The most powerful process in my observation is something I have used in therapy which I call "naming it." It involves paying attention to deep feelings, having the courage to look and see into the depth of our soul, feeling the pain, identifying it, give it a name and get a new insight. It takes being willing to open up and face it with will power.

2. This deeper level of journey requires as a first step, the achievement of challenging the early imprinting of childhood. In order to open channels to the next step which is the second layer, we need to start journey to the world of the collective unconscious, and our archetypal past that is the structure of the psyche's foundations, with many myths and stories. I have constructed a four stage developmental model for this evolutionary process.

This is commonly experienced as the very dark and mysterious underground where our deep perceptions about our womanhood or manhood come from;

specifically with regard to the roles towards the other sex and our abilities versus the other sex. There is in us a deep perception of what we really are capable of, and how we might have restricted the potentials within us.

Girls as well as boys receive all the subliminal messages from the first day of their lives. The subliminal and also straightforward messages have been coming from family, other people, history, TV programs, childhood stories, songs, movies, books, teachers, friends, etc. It's all about who we are, what we should be, what we can do or cannot do, what we should or shouldn't do, etc.

Questioning and re-evaluating all these values and beliefs that are functioning within us is vital for the sake of choosing our own values.

If you look at women around the world we can see differentiation based on the culture and other variables and how it illuminates what happens in their marital relationships, and how the relationships operate between men and women based on the symbolism that has been deeply engraved in their psyches.

In the Arab-Muslim world, women believe that if they don't cover their skin and their hair, they are damned by God. Therefore not only their bodies remain imprisoned in their Islamic cover, their souls also have been imprisoned for centuries.

This is the process of breaking from the myths that have lived in us all around the world for thousands of years. So the passage of time by itself is not going to solve this problem. The developmental process and becoming truly free is a complex one. It goes beyond our childhood; though if we don't deal with our childhood issues, we cannot even open way to the collective unconscious at the mythical, symbolic, and archetypal layers.

The thinking woman is no longer a biological object as a vehicle used for procreation, dominated by biological man, where only the biological strength spoke. Therefore she was denied any possibility for communication and negotiation. But after the physical liberation, the emotional liberation is even more complicated.

A female patient of mine who was emotionally and deeply dependent on her abusive husband to the point that she could not leave him and she had to receive years of therapeutic support in order to finally take charge of her life. Her case is an example that there are more women who suffer from abusive relationships than men.

This reminds me of the story of a woman who was emotionally and deeply dependent on her abusive husband, and she could not leave him. It is not an accident that there are more women who suffer from abusive relationships than men.

Parallel to the psycho-social developmental stages of individuals, which I spoke about in earlier chapters, I believe women and men are also going through a historical developmental process; a developmental process that every one of us in the world can find ourselves in. We now find ourselves in different places on the spectrum—a psycho-historical evolution in the relationship of the two genders.

As I indicated in earlier chapters a child takes steps toward the elementary and physical independence from its mother in early childhood and then in adolescence she or he goes through finding her or his own not yet fully developed identity by separating his/her ideas from those of his/ her parents' and attaching them to those of peers. This process can be used as an example of women earlier in 20th century America, who took steps in establishing some elementary rights in the world of men. They then rebelled in some ways in 1960-1970s by sexual liberalism and use of drugs, looking for their own, not yet quite developed identity. Going through these developmental stages women couldn't yet be happy and live seriously into symbolic adulthood, so that also changed and grew out of the 1960s and 1970s rebellion.

BECOMING A GODDESS

In the beginning chapters the emergence of Minoan culture and the goddesses were discussed. Archeologists believe that the Minoans, whose civilization lasted longer than all known civilizations, were primarily a mercantile people engaged in overseas trade. In the long history of their civilization they had a high degree of organization, without a trace of the military aristocracies that characterized others; unfortunately, it is believed that a large earthquake or a huge volcanic explosion caused the end of their civilization. With such evidence that the Minoans were a successful civilization with equal and powerful participation of women in all spheres of trade, political, social, and spiritual activities as well as in sports, we can infer that the potential and hope for present humanity is possibly a realistic one.

The following is a depiction of a woman's journey in becoming a heroine or a goddess. This is a developmental process with identifiable stages that I believe a woman can pass through in order to integrate both feminine and masculine components equally and powerfully, in her psyche and in her function in society.

THE JOURNEY

The journey of a woman to become a goddess takes her from the road that is split with its role perceptions and expectations, to an integrated self, fulfilling completeness and a powerful balance. The stages are as follows:

1. <u>Stage 1-Split Feminine</u>: The heroine in this phase is imbalanced with the undiscovered archetypal issues and has not yet found the treasures. But she has a powerful desire to face the dragons protecting the treasures. She knows that it's not an easy task to go through this journey alone and face the fears. She knows once she faces fears and fights off the dragons protecting the inner treasures, she will discover tangible strength which grants her the power of the masculine. This would be the phase where one learns how the inner conflicts and fears limit one's life. The fears loose power. More energy becomes available in the form of motivation, hope and enthusiasm.

2. <u>Stage 2-Split Masculine</u>: She touches the strength of masculine and in order to examine and learn further has to distance herself from the traditional learned feminine roles. She is still not balanced, she sees the need to stay and explore the other side (the masculine) to find the treasures and make them hers. At this point she is identifying more with masculine side and suppresses the feminine qualities including the nurturance. This is only the beginning of the journey; she is yet to equip herself with strengths and sustenance for the rest of the journey. She still does not feel the true fulfillment and completeness; something is missing; the feminine side. But in order to fight the dragons she has to equip herself with masculine qualities; one apparently has to go to the extreme in order to fully explore and learn the masculine. Perhaps this is the stage people refer to as being a feminist often with negative connotations.

3. <u>Stage 3-Healing the feminine</u>: This is the stage of rediscovering the feminine by choice, finding it not as an inferior side, but as a fulfilling part of her life. She discovers deeply, in order to own the masculine power, she doesn't need to sacrifice or repress the feminine needs and contributions. In this stage she is learning to give up the split quality of her being. She can heal the divide between the two sides and reconcile with both at the same time. However, to go through this stage requires one to heal the scars of limitations, oppression, and feelings of inferiority or dependence attributed to the feminine side. This is also the time to resolve old conflicts with her mother and father regarding the gender role representations.

4. <u>Integration and Becoming a goddess</u>: It's all discovered and fallen in place with a feeling of strength, freedom and fulfillment, knowing that one is contributing to the world as well as to the self. The spirit of goddessness in a woman is the expression of both feminine and masculine without oppression or sacrifice of either side with no conflicting consequences, being able to be both at the same time. This I call the state of balance.

While it may appear naïve to assume that if and when women of the world go through this journey collectively, the world would be a balanced and peaceful place, yet it is the key to the evolutionary development for men as well. Men also need to go through a mirror image of such a journey. However, if women take the initiative at a global level, only then, historically, can men also find themselves in their own journey.

LIST OF RESOURCES

Adler, A. (1973) *The Practice and Theory of Individual Psychology*. New York, NY: Rowman & Littlefield Publishers, Inc.

Applegarth, A. (1976) *Psychic Energy Reconsidered. Journal of the American Psychoanalytic Association*. New York, NY. American Psychoanalytic Association.

Applewhite, A. (1997) Cutting Loose: *Why Women Who End Their Marriages Do So* Well. New York, NY. HarperCollins Publishers, Inc.

Bigler, R.S. (1995) *The role of classification skill in moderating environmental influences on children's gender stereotyping: A study of the functional use of gender in the classroom. Child Development*, 1995, 66,1072-1087. Austin, TX: Society for Research in Child Development, Inc.

EL Fadl, K. (2007). The Great Theft. Harper. San Francisco.

Erikson, E. (1959). *Identity and the Life Cycle; Selected Papers*. New York: International Universities Press.

Evans, S.B. (1999) Women Who Broke All the Rules: *How the Choices of a Generation Changed Our Lives.* Naperville, IL. Sourcebooks, Inc.

Frankel; Rathvon. (1980) *Whatever Happened to Cinderella?* New York, NY: St. Martin's Press.

Habermas, J. (1989). *The Structural Transformation of the Public Sphere: An Inquiry into a Category of Bourgeois Society.* Cambridge MA: The MIT Press.

Horner; Walsh. (1981) *The Psychology of Women.* New Haven, CT: Yale University Press.

Horney, K (1937). *The neurotic personality of our time.* New York: Norton.

Horney, K (1939). *New ways in psychoanalysis.* New York: Norton.

Horney, K (1942). *Self-analysis.* New York: Norton.

Horney, K (1945). *Our inner conflicts.* New York: Norton.

Horney, K (1950). *Neurosis and human growth.* New York: Norton.

Horney, K (1967). *Feminine psychology,* Ed. H. Kelman. New York: Norton.

Jackson, S. (1993). Women's Studies, New York University Press: New York.

Jung, C. (1933). *Modern Man in Search of a Soul.* London, UK: Routledge & Kegan Paul.

Kanefield, L. (1985) *Psychoanalytic Constructions of Female Development and Women's Conflicts About Achievement. Part I. Journal of American Academy of Psychoanalysis,* 13:229-246. CA. Psychoanalytic Electronic Publishing.

Miller, J.B. (1976) *Toward a New Psychology of Women.* Boston,MA: Beacon Press.

Miller, J.B. (1981) *Inequality and women's mental health: an overview.* Arlington,VA: American Psychiatric Publishing, Inc.

Rubin, L.B. (1984) *Intimate Strangers: Men and Women Together.* New York, NY. HarperCollins Publishers, Inc.

Stiver, I. (1991). *Women's growth in connection: Writings from the Stone Center.* New York; Guilford Press.

Tavris, C. & Wade, C. (1994) *Psychology in Perspective.* Reading, A: Addison-Wesley.

Tolle, E. (2005). A New Earth: *Awakening To Your Life's Purpose.* London, UK: Penguin Group.